NOT YOU AGAIN

AN ENEMIES TO LOVERS ROMANTIC COMEDY

TARA CRESCENT

FREE STORY OFFER

Get a free story when you subscribe to <u>my mailing list</u>!

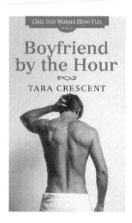

Boyfriend by the Hour

This steamy, romantic story contains a dominant hero who's pretending to be an escort, and a sassy heroine who's given up on real relationships.

Sadie:

I can't believe I have the hots for an escort.

Cole Mitchell is ripped, bearded, sexy and dominant. When he moves next door to me, I find it impossible to resist sampling the wares.

But Cole's not a one-woman kind of guy, and I won't share.

Cole:

She thinks I'm an escort. I'm not.

I thought I'd do anything to sleep with Sadie. Then I realized I want more. I want Sadie. Forever.

I'm not the escort she thinks I am.

Now, I just have to make sure she never finds out.

Cover design by Kasmit Covers. http://www.kasmitcovers.com.

NOT YOU AGAIN

She hates me with a passion of a thousand burning suns. I want her more than I've ever wanted anyone in my life. Something's got to give.

Dakota Wilde. Stubborn, impossible, perfect. A year ago, we had a smokin' hot one-night-stand. **I wanted more.** *She blew me off.* That's just the way life is, right? You don't always get everything you want.
Except I don't lose.

The chemistry between us burns hotter than a
five-alarm fire.
And when we're together, we can't seem to stop touching each other.
Our banter is heavy on the innuendo. I call Dakota my darling bratwust. She can't stop talking about my salami.

I make her laugh. She makes me a better person.

Then the town of Madison pits us against each other in an insane contest to win a restaurant permit.

I know what I have to do.

I'm not playing for the permit. *I'm playing for Dakota.* **This time, I intend to win.**

1

DAKOTA

The first person I see Monday morning is Julian King.

Ugh.

It's the last week of April. It's cold. Spring has decided to take an extended nap, and winter has us firmly in its icy fangs. The sky is overcast, and the air has that kind of dampness that clamps around you and goes through you, chilling every bone in your body. I want to go back home, wrap myself from head to toe in warmth, and swim in a vat of hot chocolate.

Unaffected by the grey skies and the bitter chill, Julian King, Madison's newest full-time resident, jogs along the beach.

Gah.

His long legs effortlessly chew up the distance. His full-sleeved t-shirt hugs his broad chest. Wide shoulders, flat stomach. Six pack abs, if my memory serves me correctly, and unfortunately, where Julian King is concerned, my memory is happy to throw forward image after image of his perfect, naked body.

Did I say ugh already? *Ugh.*

Sherri Stephenson comes out of Fannie's, bundled up in a puffy red coat. She stares at Julian and then turns ruefully to me. "If I were twenty years younger..." she says. "Hell, even ten years younger. You know what I mean?"

She gives me an expectant look, and I realize she's waiting for me to respond.

Say something blandly pleasant about Julian, Dakota.

Nothing comes to mind. I draw a complete blank. My brain contemplates the idea of paying Julian King a compliment and mounts a rebellion. Hell, no.

"If you like the type," I mutter grudgingly.

Sherri raises an eyebrow. "What type? Handsome, polite, and successful?"

I snort. "Oh, please. It's a cunning mask. Julian King would sell his grandmother to the wolves if it gained him a sliver of an advantage."

Like he did with me. This time last year, Julian King *deliberately* let me assume he lived in Toronto. He *deliberately* led me to believe that he was a safe target for a one-night stand. He was hot, funny, and charming, and he smooth-talked his way into my bed.

Then I found out the jerk quit his big-city lawyer job, moved to Madison, and founded his gourmet sausage company.

He's called his business Sausage King. The normally conservative residents of Madison should have been up in arms at the name, but no. They think it's funny.

Funny.

Gah.

Would I have slept with Julian if I'd known he was about to move to Madison? *Hell no.* Everybody here is a gossip, and I prefer not to give anyone any ammunition. Been there, done that, no desire for a repeat. The town's still talking about the way my father abandoned my mother, and that had happened twenty years ago. I'll never forget the sly whispers, the looks of pity, the casseroles our neighbors brought as a pretext to visit so they could interrogate her about what happened.

To this day, the smell of tuna casserole turns my stomach.

My brother Dominic had left Madison for a few years. Me? I hadn't wanted to leave. The moment I finished college, I came right back. Gossip aside, I love it here. I love the beach. I love walking along the water and sinking my toes into hot sand. During shoulder season, I can wake up at the crack of dawn and take my canoe out, and there's not a single person around for miles. Despite its flaws, Madison will always be home to me.

Sherri looks shocked at my remark. Too late, I realize what I said. *Idiot, Dakota.* Nothing will fire up the gossip mills like the rumor of a feud between Julian and me. "Don't mind me, Sherri. I'm always cranky before coffee. I have to agree; Julian is pretty easy on the eyes."

There. I said that out loud without gagging. I should get a prize.

Thankfully, Sherri buys my explanation. "I think I'll put together a fundraising calendar for Madison next year. I'll get all the young men in the area to pose shirtless for it. Julian, Dominic, Zach Janssen over in Bainbridge..." Her voice trails off as she contemplates the sad lack of eligible men in Madison, but nothing can keep Sherri down for long. She perks up again and winks at me. "For charity, of course."

"Of course." My voice is dry. I'm trying to think of how to

extract myself from this excruciating conversation when the worst thing in the world happens.

Julian King sees us staring at him.

The asshole's smirk widens. That stupidly sexy dimple on his chin deepens, and he lifts his arm in a smug wave.

Cocky jackass.

If Monday morning is any indication, this is going to be a stellar week.

I'M STANDING in line at the coffee shop, waiting for the tourist family in front of me to decide what they want, when I feel a familiar presence at my back. "Well, well, well."

It's Julian King. Speak of the devil, and he appears.

His smug drawl sets my teeth on edge. I whirl around and tilt my head up to glare at him.

It has no effect. His grin widens. "Checking me out, are you, Wilde?" His grin widens. "I get it; you can't take your eyes off me. Like what you see?"

He's standing too close, waiting for me to draw away. The jerk is baiting me, and I'd be damned if I'm going to give him the satisfaction. For a second, I'm tempted to tell Julian what I really think of him, but there are kids around, and parents get pretty touchy when I swear around their precious bundles of joy. "I was hoping you'd hit a patch of ice and fall flat on your face," I tell him, my voice perfectly polite. "Pity it didn't happen. Still, I live in hope."

His teeth flash. "Sure you do, Wilde." His eyes trail down my body, his inspection slow and thorough. He'd looked at me like this a year ago. Later, in bed, his hands and mouth had delivered on every promise his eyes had made, and then some.

Should have never slept with him, Dakota.

"Had a hard time fitting that massive ego of yours through the door?" The instant I bite out those words, I suppress my groan. *Idiot. You gave him one hell of an opening.*

Of course, Julian King takes advantage. His eyes dance with amusement, and his voice lowers to a seductive simmer. "It's not my massive ego you're thinking about, are you?" He takes a half-step closer, heat just pouring off his body, and it takes all the willpower I have to stand my ground. "Anytime you want the king again, sweetness, you just have to ask."

The king? The guy's given his cock a name? Egotistical bastard. I picture wrapping my hands around his neck and squeezing. It's a good image. "Why would I?" I ask coolly. "It wasn't that memorable."

"Not memorable? You moaned out my name, Dakota. You shuddered through orgasm after orgasm on my tongue. You woke me up in the middle of the night with your mouth on my dick, and then you climbed on top of me and rode me until you came again." He takes in my too-flushed cheeks and male satisfaction flares in his eyes. "You don't remember any of that? Because I do."

At least he kept his voice down. "Fuck you, King," I clench out between ground teeth.

"Like I said, anytime you want, sweetness. You know where I live."

I give him my most quelling expression. "Hell will freeze over first."

If I'm hoping my words put a dent in that puffed-up ego, they're promptly dashed to the ground. Julian just chuckles, as unflappable as ever. "You're up," he says helpfully. "Hurry up, won't you? Some of us have places to be and things to do."

I look up. The tourist family is long gone, and Leela

Ahuja, the teenager who works the morning shift at the coffee shop on Mondays, Wednesdays, and Thursdays, is staring at the two of us, her mouth open.

Damn it. What the hell is wrong with me today? First Sherri, and now Leela. The news will be around town in an hour. In prime tourist season, there might be a whisper of a chance that everyone's too busy to gossip. In shoulder season, like now? Not a prayer. Leela will tell her mother Mina, who sits on the town council and runs a yoga retreat slash bed-and-breakfast. Mina plays poker every week with Manuel Medina. Manuel is good friends with my entire family. Ten to one, my mother calls me before the end of the day, asking me if I'm dating Julian. She will tell me things about motherhood and ticking biological clocks and how I'm not getting any younger.

Ninety-five percent of the time, Sandra Flanagan is a progressive feminist who does not believe that a woman needs a man to be happy. But one of her painter friends' daughter just gave birth, and Margie brought around pictures of the newborn baby, thus sealing my fate. My mother has grandbaby fever.

"Oh please," I hiss through clenched teeth. I just bought the property next to me. I've put down a fifty-thousand-dollar deposit so I can expand Dakota's Pizza. I've got contractors to hire, ovens to install, and furniture to buy. He thinks he's busy? Cocky asshole. "We both know that the only thing you have to do with your day is playing with your tiny sausage." I turn to Leela and paste a smile on my face. "I'll have a large cappuccino to go."

"I'll have the same thing, Leela," Julian chimes in, his voice dancing with laughter. "And one of your chocolate chip muffins. Put Dakota's drink on my bill, please." I turn back to tell him that's not necessary, and I see a spark light in his eyes. "Coffee powers her broomstick."

Ooh.

Forget strangling. It's far too quick. I'm going to make a Julian King doll and stab it with a pin. In the nuts. Over and over again.

2

JULIAN

Ocean blue eyes that look ready to emit fire. A tongue so sharp it would cut glass. Curves that won't quit. I thought I liked peaceful, low maintenance women. Then I met Dakota Wilde.

Drinking my cappuccino, I make my way back to my cottage to *play with my tiny sausage,* as Dakota so charmingly put it. I spend a few pleasant minutes fantasizing about Dakota taking me up on my offer and sleeping with me again. Then I realize I'm wallowing and banish her from my mind.

Stubborn, irritating woman.

Last Victoria Day weekend, I'd attended Vicki and Cat's brewpub opening with Zach, Penny, and a couple other friends. I'd seen Dakota there.

There's no doubt about it—it was lust at first sight. The chemistry was off-the-charts good. We'd both felt it. I'd wanted to rip her clothes off. She wanted to do the same to me.

And we did. It was memorable. Hot. Passionate.

It had also been just the one night.

Not my choice. She'd sneaked off at dawn, and when I sent her a text message the day after, she'd ignored it. I'd sent her another message; she hadn't responded to that one either.

Message received. I thought we had one-in-a-lifetime chemistry, the kind that was worth exploring, but clearly, it was all from my end. To Dakota, it was nothing more than a one-night stand.

Wallowing again, King.

To stop myself from thinking about Dakota, I focus my thoughts on Sausage King. Last May, I'd quit my job with nothing more than a vague dream of starting a small business. A year later, Sausage King, my artisanal sausage company supplies thirty bars and restaurants all over the peninsula. It's getting to the point where I'm seriously considering hiring a couple of workers to ease the load. I've set targets, and I'm ahead of them.

I'm ready for the next challenge.

I walk down Front Street and turn on Harbor. Most of the retail businesses in Madison are located on these two streets. Front runs east-west and parallels the beach, and Harbor runs north-south. I pass the unimaginatively named Madison Motel, the Shipwreck Fish Fry, Clancy's Canoe Rental, and Beth Shepperd's ice cream store, The Frozen Spoon.

The Frozen Spoon shows no signs of life.

Huh. That's interesting.

I stop to take a look. Even at best of times, The Frozen Spoon didn't do a ton of business, which is shocking, really, when you consider that it's selling excellent handmade ice-cream in a beach town. But it's not hard to see why. Unlike its neighbors, the store is set back on the property, and people have to wander down a driveway to reach the entrance. It's also in terrible shape. The roof needs to be replaced. The paint is peeling. The stair rails look like they'd yield if I put any weight on them.

If I ran the place, I'd fix it up. Then I'd add a deck out front, so tourists would have a place to sit down. I'd expand the offerings, serving not just ice-cream, but also food. Nothing fancy, nothing that requires a commercial kitchen. Grilled cheese sandwiches, salads, sausages, that kind of thing...

Sausages.

The back of my neck prickles.

Beth Shepperd is sixty-six. Her husband Jim died unexpectedly last year. According to the gossips, she doesn't have enough money to renovate. Banks won't give her a loan because they don't consider the business a good risk.

I think I've just found my next challenge.

I stride down the driveway. I'm halfway to the front when Mrs. Shepperd opens her door. "We're closed," she calls out.

Yeah, that part is obvious. "Hello, Mrs. Shepperd." I give her my best winning smile, the smile I used to save for judges when I made my closing statement. "My name is Julian King. I'm Candace King's grandson."

Only in Madison is my dead grandmother more of a celebrity than I am. Mrs. Shepperd's puzzled expression clears. "Of course. You're the guy who makes sausages. You're living in her cottage now, aren't you?"

"I am," I confirm, my trust-me smile still in place. A woman I dated once called it the kind of smile a shark gives you before he gnaws into your flesh. She hadn't meant it as a compliment. "Do you have a few minutes? I'd like to talk to you about your store."

Her eyes narrow. "Is something the problem? Town

council has already harassed me about the paint and the garden." She shivers as a cold blast of wind hits us. "I told Roger that I can't afford the fines. As soon as it warms up, I'll mow the lawn."

The lawn? It's the end of April. Why the fuck does the city care about her lawn? Yes, Mrs. Shepperd's garden looks scraggly, but it's hardly the worst offender.

Then I register the rest of her comment. Roger Wexler. Of course. Sounds like the real estate developer wants to expand his holdings, and the way he's going to do it is by harassing Mrs. Shepperd.

Asshole.

"I'm not from the town council, Mrs. Shepperd. Let me guess. Roger Wexler made an offer for The Frozen Spoon."

She sighs. "How did you know? Yes, Roger wants to buy it." Her expression is sad. "This used to be my mother's house, and her mother's before that. It's been in our family for generations. I don't want to sell, but I don't think I have a choice. Samuel works in the city, and his wife's been diagnosed with breast cancer. Even if he wanted to help, he can't."

Samuel must be her son. "If you don't mind me asking, how much did he offer?"

"One-fifty. I know it's low, but Roger said he'd need to spend thousands of dollars to bring this place up to code." She sighs again. "I'm behind on my tax payments. Jim used to handle it, you know? The CRA sent me a bill in March for twenty-five thousand dollars. I have to fix the stairs before I can open this season, and I have to add a wheelchair ramp. I just can't afford it."

One hundred and fifty thousand. Outrage stiffens my spine. Yes, the building is in rough shape, but the land alone is worth at least double that, and Wexler knows it. The douchebag is taking advantage of Mrs. Shepperd.

Aren't you planning to do the same thing? My conscience prompts.

I quell that voice. I'm an ex-lawyer; I've had a lot of practice ignoring my conscience. "Have you signed anything?"

"No, not yet."

Yes! Excellent. "Mrs. Shepperd, I'd like to make a counter-offer," I tell her. "Unlike Roger Wexler, I'll pay fair market value. Three-fifty if I can take possession at the start of July."

If I'm to get the place open before summer's over, I'll have to start construction almost immediately. First, the wheelchair ramp and the stairs. Then the deck, and finally, give the entire place a coat of paint.

I stopped by the Frozen Spoon last year. From what I can remember, the interior shouldn't need much work. I can slap on a coat of paint for the moment, and work on refinishing the hard wood floors and moving the interior walls during winter.

If I hustle, I can get the restaurant open by the first of August.

Mrs. Shepperd stares at me, her mouth open. "Three hundred and fifty thousand dollars?" she says, sounding dazed. "Two hundred thousand dollars more than Roger Wexler."

Unlike Wexler, I don't cheat defenseless old ladies. "The Frozen Spoon is in a great location. I'm willing to pay a premium for it."

I'm already making a to-do list. Ben Watanabe did my commercial kitchen last year, on time and on budget. I don't know what his schedule looks like, but I'll need to get on it as soon as possible. The deck is a must-have.

The stairs and the ramp, I can probably do myself. I've been practicing my handyman skills by renovating my grandmother's cottage. I need to drive to the city tomorrow for meat anyway; I'll add a stop at a hardware store to buy lumber for the project. I could begin work as early as Wednesday.

I open my mouth to ask Mrs. Shepperd how quickly we can move, and then I take in her expression. Half-shocked, half-saddened. I remember what she said. This property has been in her family for generations, and both Wexler and I are circling it like sharks sensing prey.

Julian, for fuck's sake, don't rush the old lady.

I soften my voice. "Take some time to think about it," I encourage Mrs. Shepperd. "Talk to your son, talk to your friends and your lawyer. I can have the papers drawn up tomorrow. I'd like to open this summer. But there's no real hurry. I'll leave the offer open until the end of summer."

She nods wordlessly.

I'm still a shark. "If it's okay with you, I'll stop by on Wednesday and fix your stairs and install a wheelchair ramp," I add. "With the ramp in place, you can open this weekend."

Her eyes narrow. "Let me guess. You'll charge me for your time if I decide not to sell?"

"Not at all." There's a time for the stick, and a time for the carrot. The real art is knowing what to use when. "I've no doubt that when Roger Wexler hears my bid, he'll counter. He won't offer three-fifty, but maybe he'll remind you that he's on the town council, and he can make your life miserable if he chooses." I give her a steady look. Mrs. Shepperd isn't a fool; she knows I have ulterior motives. In situations like this, a little honesty goes a long way. "I want you to sell to me, Mrs. Shepperd. The ramp is a goodwill gesture."

She looks at me for a long time. I wait. I have endless reserves of patience.

Finally, she inclines her head. "When you come by on Wednesday," she says. "Bring the papers. I'll take a look."

We shake on it. I walk away, anticipation adding a spring in my step. I'm about to be Madison's newest restaurateur.

Brace yourself. The Sausage King has arrived.

3

DAKOTA

Dakota's Pizza is closed on Mondays. Doesn't mean I don't work. I march to my office, seething with indignation at Julian's comment. *Coffee powers her broomstick.*

He thinks I'm a witch? Puh-leeze. He hasn't seen anything yet.

Admit it, Dakota. It was pretty funny.

I catch up with a week's worth of paperwork. Invoices, orders, payroll, shift schedules—all of this gets done on Mondays. Normally, I power through the backlog quickly and am done by lunch, leaving me the rest of the day to do with what I will.

Not so today. Over and over, my mind keeps returning to Julian, to his sexy, smug smile.

You moaned out my name, Dakota.

Yes, I did.

You shuddered through orgasm after orgasm on my tongue.

Guilty as charged.

Anytime you want the king again, sweetness, you just have to ask.

Never. The nerve of the man. Yes, the sex was good—okay, fine, the sex was the best I've ever had—but that doesn't mean I'm going to crawl back into his bed. For one thing, he's just too goddamn confident it's only a matter of time before we sleep together again. I don't really play games, but I resent his assumption that I'm a sure thing.

My stomach growls loudly. I look at the time on my computer and stifle a curse. It's twelve-thirty. I'm supposed to be done, and I still have another hour of work left. I can't stop thinking about Julian.

Stupid Sausage King.

This won't do at all. I need distraction, stat.

I get to my feet and head over to the Madison Brewpub. Like Dakota's Pizza, the brewpub is also closed on Mondays. Vicki's is seated at a table, typing something on her laptop. Cat, my soon-to-be sister-in-law is in the back, fiddling with a dial on one of the brewing tanks.

Vicki looks up when I walk in. "Is it lunchtime already?" she asks with a groan. "Crap. I am so behind this morning."

"You're not the only one." I pull up a chair and wave to Cat, who waves back and holds up three fingers. Yeah, right. Three minutes my ass. I know Cat. When she's in the middle of brewing something, she forgets to eat. In ten minutes, Vicki and I will have to drag her out. "Do either of you have time to take a break?"

"Sorry, you can't have my fiancée." My brother Dominic walks in, his clothes covered, as usual, in a thin layer of sawdust. "I'm kidnapping her."

Cat looks up and beams with pleasure. "Dom," she calls out. "What are you doing here?"

"You forgot to eat breakfast again, kit cat."

"Crap, you're right." She stops what she's doing and joins

us in the front, standing on tiptoe to kiss Dominic. "I left the sandwich you packed me on the counter, didn't I? Sorry."

He shrugs. "I put it away. Do you have time for lunch? I've got to head to Marmet for a delivery. Want to come? We can stop at that Italian place you like on the way."

"Yes please," Cat says promptly. "Sorry, Vicki, Dakota. When my fiancé says jump..."

I roll my eyes. "The two of you are sickeningly cute," I tell them. "Have you set a date for the wedding yet?"

Cat shakes her head. "Maybe at the end of summer, once the tourists are gone. It'll be pretty low-key." She takes off her apron and shakes out her hair. "See you two later."

I watch them leave, feeling kind of doleful. They're in a relationship, and they're really great together. Good for Dominic. I thought the two of us were scarred forever because of our father, but I was wrong. Last year, Dom had met Cat, and practically right from the start, he seemed to know that she was the one.

They're a fantastic couple. They're supportive, they make each other laugh, they help each other out. It's almost enough to give me commitment fever.

You climbed on top of me and rode me until you came again. You don't remember any of that? Because I do.

Stop it, Dakota. That's just sex. Don't confuse it with anything else.

I can't fall in love. I can't afford it. After my father left, my mother hadn't dated for almost twenty years. She's just started going out with Tim Pollard, who has been crazy about her for longer than I can remember.

As much as I want to pretend that I have nothing in common with Sandra Flanigan, we're identical in this. I still can't think of my father without reliving the pain I felt when

I realized he wasn't coming back. My mom and I, we love too deeply to risk our hearts.

I date casually; I have discreet one-night stands. I just won't risk heartbreak. It's a decision that's served me well. Dakota's Pizza is doing well enough that I can afford to expand. I've bought the place next door. My focus is on my business, and that's just the way I like it.

I drag my attention back to Vicki. Her expression is wistful. "When's Liam coming up?" I ask her. Liam is Vicki's boyfriend. The two of them have been in a long-distance relationship for over a year. "I haven't seen him around lately."

"He's not. We broke up."

Ah, crap. "I'm sorry, Vicki. Do you want to talk about it?"

She shrugs. "It was probably always doomed. I just didn't let myself see it. I assumed Liam would move to Madison, even though he never gave me a sign he wanted to leave Toronto. I thought that he because he was a writer, he could work from anywhere. I finally came out and asked him if a move was even on the cards, and he said no. We should have had the conversation nine months ago, but I didn't want to hurt his feelings and he didn't want to hurt mine." She grimaces. "Of course, that's what we ended up doing."

"Are you okay?"

"I will be." She sighs. "The thing is, I get it. I understand why Liam doesn't want to move away from Toronto. Some days, I miss the city so much that it hurts."

I didn't know Vicki was having regrets about moving to Madison. "It's been a long winter," I say carefully. "I went stir crazy in February. And it still hasn't warmed up."

"It's not the weather. The snow didn't help, but that's not it. I miss sushi. I miss walking out my door and being stumbling distance to three amazing pho restaurants. In Toronto, when I wanted curry at two in the morning, I knew where to go. I miss the rhythm of the city. The pace, the energy."

"Does Cat know how you feel?"

Vicki nods. "Yes, I've told her. I want to sell my stake in the business. I would sell it to Cat, but she has no interest in being a restaurateur. She likes brewing; she doesn't want to run the front of the house." She looks up at me. "I've been meaning to broach the topic. I thought you might be interested."

"Me?"

"Yeah. It makes sense, doesn't it? Cat's marrying your brother; the two of you are going to be related. You already get along. You know Madison like the back of your hand, and you have a ton of restaurant experience. You bought the place next door. If you managed this place too, you could convert all three restaurants into one interconnected space."

Ooh. That's an attractive vision. For a second, I'm seriously tempted, and then reality intervenes. "I can't swing it anytime soon," I say regretfully. "I put a fifty-grand deposit on the place next door. Until it's up and running, I won't have any money."

"That's fine," Vicki replies. "I'm not in a huge hurry. I don't want to stay here forever, but I'm not going to screw Cat over. She's the one who will be in a partnership with whoever I sell to, not me. We talked. She has the right of refusal on anyone who might be interested. I won't sell unless she's satisfied."

Could I make it work? I'd be overextended, but it's still a tempting proposition. Real estate on Front Street is impossibly hard to acquire. The Madison Brewpub is popular. An opportunity like this might never come my way again. "Are you considering anyone else?"

"You're the obvious first choice," she says. "But I thought that if you weren't interested, I might ask Julian."

I grit my teeth. "Julian King?" *Trust the jackass to worm his way into Vicki's good books.*

"Yeah. He already supplies our sausages. He's a fast learner, smart as hell, and he gets along pretty well with both Cat and Dom."

Ugh. I try to imagine Julian working at the Madison Brewpub. Every time I walk into my restaurant, I'll risk seeing him. Every time I leave, he'll be there, smirking his smug male smile, flashing that sexy dimple, tempting me with his hard body.

As it is, a year after our hookup, I can't get him out of my mind. I haven't even been on a date since I slept with him.

The idea of him being right next door, all the time? *I can't let that happen.*

"I'm definitely interested."

Vicki gives me a curious look. "Dakota, do you not like Julian? Is there something I should know?"

"What do you mean?" I ask warily. Damn it. Vicki won't gossip, but I should still conceal my emotions better. First Sherri, then Leela, and now Vicki. So far, I'm zero for three.

"Well, you slept with him the day of our opening, didn't you? The two of you couldn't take your eyes off each other, and you left at the same time. I just assumed..." Her voice trails off and a rueful look fills her face. "I'm getting as bad as everyone else here."

Not really. Vicki, whatever her other faults are, doesn't gossip. If I tell her a secret, I can pretty much guarantee it'll stay that way.

"Yeah, I slept with Julian. It was just the one night."

"Then he moved to Madison, and you do your best to avoid him. You can't say a single nice thing about him." She leans forward, a concerned look on her face. "Did he do anything he shouldn't have? Say the word, and we'll find a different supplier."

She's asking me if Julian sexually assaulted me.

I can't stand the asshole. He's cocky and arrogant. Every time he smiles his smug smile, my fingers itch. I want to slap the smirk off his face.

"No, of course not. I was a willing participant." A *very* willing participant.

She looks at me curiously. "What's the deal with the two of you?" Her eyes twinkle. "Was the sex awful? Tell me everything."

"Everything?"

I haven't been able to talk to anyone about my one-night stand with Julian. There are lots of women I'm friendly with, but if I tell them, word will get around.

But Vicki won't talk.

"Every single sordid detail." She rubs her palms together in anticipation. "Did he hum during sex? Did he thump his chest and call himself the champion after he came? Did he obsessively dab himself with hand sanitizer? Did he ask you to rate his performance?"

I burst out laughing. "Tell me you're making these things up."

She shakes her head. "Sadly, no. I slept with the hummer."

I have to know. "What song did he hum?"

"Cotton Eye Joe," she replies, deadpan. "He thrust in rhythm to the chorus. It was surreal."

I'm laughing so hard I almost choke. "No way. You're joking."

"I'm dead serious. Now it's your turn. How was the sex?"

How can I describe my night with Julian King? "Have you ever done cocaine?"

Vicki's eyes widen. "No, have you?"

"Are you kidding? Can you imagine my mother's reaction? No, my roommate in freshman year of college did coke. She would go on and on about how great it was. According to Christina, when she took a hit, every sense was heightened. She said she felt everything, and everything was euphoria and excitement. She called it a rush of intense pleasure, so intense that she didn't think her body could bear it." I take a deep breath. "That's what sex with Julian was like."

It's the first time I've admitted that out loud.

Vicki whistles through her teeth. "Well, damn. Why aren't you taking another hit?"

"Because he's like cocaine, Vicki. One hit, and he's rearranged your body chemistry, and you're addicted. Sure, the high is great, but the crash?" I shake my head. "I don't do drugs, and I don't do Julian King."

Vicki frowns at me. "You're so cynical. You shouldn't be. I don't know if Julian is the right guy for you, but neither will you if you don't give him a chance. Even now, fresh off my breakup with Liam, as miserable as I am, I know that my heart will heal and when it does, I'll be ready to search again. I want what Dom and Cat have."

Time to change the topic. "Are you going to let Liam know you're planning to move back to Toronto?"

"No. That relationship ran its course." She forces a smile on her face. "Okay, I have one last question about Julian. Did the Sausage King measure up?"

Vicki has no filter. It's one of the things I like best about her. "Really? We're going to talk about size?"

"Hell, yes. Length, girth, circumcised or not, give me the

gory details. I just broke up with Liam. I need all the distraction I can get."

I'm not easily prone to embarrassment, but my cheeks are flaming. "I refuse to describe Julian King's penis," I say with dignity. "But I will say one thing. He was hung like a horse."

A throat clears. I look up, aghast, and meet Julian's laughing brown eyes. "Hung like a horse," he repeats, his voice absolutely dripping with male satisfaction. "Why, thank you, Dakota."

Kill me. Kill me now.

4

JULIAN

Hung like a horse.

I'm practically whistling as I drive back to my cottage. To think, I almost hired a driver to handle deliveries. Dakota might have snarled at me, but there's no denying she'd said it.

I'm grinning like an idiot as I pull into my driveway. Skipping the house, I head to the commercial kitchen in the back. I've sunk an astonishing amount of money into this place, and it shows. Gleaming stainless steel is everywhere. Walk-in cooling unit, industrial freezer, refrigerated line station, industrial range hood... the list goes on and on.

It's worth every penny I spent.

It's almost four. I pull out my phone to check my messages. There's a voicemail from Mildred Bower at the Legion. "Julian, could we order two hundred of the kielbasa Sidney Granger liked for our Victoria Day barbecue?"

I can't remember what Sid Granger sampled; it was four weeks ago. Checking my notes, I see that it was *serdelki,* the Polish equivalent to a frankfurter.

The barbecue is to raise funds to buy the local hospital

an MRI machine. I call Mrs. Bower back and confirm the order. "It's on the house," I tell her. "Just doing my part for the community."

She sounds thrilled. "Thank you so much, Julian. That's really kind of you."

I grimace. I'm not doing it out of the goodness of my heart; donating the sausages is good PR. It's a sound business decision, that's all.

I'm learning from the best. Dakota's Pizza is extremely involved in the community. Dakota is not only generous with her money, but she's also lavish with her time. She volunteers at the senior center. She serves on the library board. Everyone likes her. Everyone trusts her.

Me? I spent six years as a litigator. People see me as a necessary evil. And of course, nobody trusts lawyers. Then again, given that I'm plotting about how to use the Legion's fundraiser as free publicity for the Sausage King, they're probably onto something.

I finish my conversation with Mildred Bower. Almost as soon as I hang up, my phone rings again. I pick it up.

"How's the Sausage King these days?"

I grin. Ward Lewington is one of my oldest friends. "I don't go around calling myself that." Honesty compels me to alter that statement. "Most of the time."

Ward groans. "Tell me you didn't walk up to a woman and use either 'sausage' or 'king' as a pickup line, Julian."

I open my refrigerator and take stock of the empty shelves. I'm going to have to make a meat run soon. I'm running low on supplies. Madison is a grocery wasteland; I'll have to head into the city this week. "I'd tell you that, but I'd be lying. In my defense, it wasn't exactly a pickup line. I was trying to annoy someone."

"Dakota." The amusement in his voice comes through

clearly. "It's Dakota, isn't it?"

A year ago, I'd made the mistake of mentioning Dakota to Ward. Should have known better. The guy has a mind like a steel trap. "To what do I owe the pleasure of this call?" I ask, ignoring his question. "If you're calling to whine about your love life, you already know what I'm going to say. Tell Dixie how you feel about her."

"Dix is dating someone else, remember?"

I'm an ex-lawyer. Ruthlessness is in my blood. "She's dating Charles Blumenthal. The guy is a waste of space. Break them up."

Ward doesn't bite. "I'm not going to do that."

"You'd prefer to be miserable watching them together? They've been dating for three years. Any moment now, Blumenthal is going to pop the question. You know that."

He sucks in a breath. Guilt pinches at me. "Sorry."

"That's okay. You're right." I hear the resignation in his voice and feel like a jerk. "I called to catch up. Tell me how the business is doing."

"Pretty good. I'm cash-flow positive."

"Already?" Ward whistles. "Nice job. I'm assuming you're depreciating the kitchen expense?"

Ward's an accountant, and a pretty good one. "Yeah, I am. The kitchen cost a hundred and fifty grand. It'll take the business at least five years to pay it off."

He snorts. "Pay off what? You didn't get a loan for it. What was the size of your last bonus check?"

I start making a shopping list as I chat with Ward. "Fair enough. This isn't an expensive hobby though. I want Sausage King to be a viable business."

"Let me guess," he says. "You think it's going to make your parents respect your decision to quit law."

My hand freezes in the air. I tighten my grip on the pen.

"I'm thirty-four. I don't need my parents' approval to do anything."

"Doesn't mean you don't want it," Ward says pointedly.

He needs to drop this topic. My parents are a sore spot. "I also made a verbal offer on a failing ice-cream store. I'm thinking of opening a restaurant."

Ward laughs out loud. "Of course, you are. Only you, Julian. You quit BCF because you were done working a hundred hours a week. Instead of going the safe route and joining some Fortune 500 company's corporate counsel, you decided you were going to make sausages." He chuckles. "You were going to relax, you told me. Instead, the second you've hit your first milestone, you're already taking on something new. Have you ever considered doing less, not more?"

I wince. I'd said the same thing to my father last January. He'd had a bad cancer scare. He'd sworn that he was going to prioritize his family, not work. For three years, he went through radiation, chemo, the works. Then, the instant the doctors gave him a clean bill of health, he was back to working eighty hours a week.

The job is a drug, and he can't give it up.

Fredrick King's cancer diagnosis had made me reexamine my own life. But am I making his mistakes all over again?

"I might be a little Type A."

"You think?" he asks dryly. "Also, a failing ice-cream store in a beach town? That's not possible, is it?"

"You'd be surprised. Beth Shepperd is in her sixties. Her husband died unexpectedly. He did their taxes. She's behind on payment, has no money to fix the place up, can't get a loan either, and, unless she gets a wheelchair ramp installed, she can't open for the season."

"Julian, you're robbing an old lady."

Guilt stabs me again. "Hey," I protest. "I'm paying a fair market price."

"You're taking advantage of a cash flow crisis." Ward sounds disapproving.

"Roger Wexler is taking advantage of a cash flow crisis, not me." I can't keep the defensiveness out of my voice. "He lowballed Mrs. Shepperd. He offered to pay one hundred and fifty thousand dollars for a property that's worth double that. I countered with three-fifty. I'm not the villain in this story, Ward."

"If you say so. On a different note, what are you doing Victoria Day weekend?"

Wallowing in misery, probably.

I just don't understand Dakota. We'd been great together, and no, I'm not blowing smoke up my ass. If the sex was bad, we wouldn't have done it over and over again that night. For the life of me, I can't figure out why she left in the middle of the night, why she blew me off the day after, and why she's so snippy every time she sees me.

Four times.

Four bone-shattering orgasms.

I shouldn't tease her. I shouldn't verbally spar with her every time I see her. I'm like a kid in kindergarten, pulling on the pigtails of the girl I like. It's juvenile and demented.

"Nothing, really. You want to come down? There's plenty of room here, and I have a refrigerator filled with beer."

"You sure? Cause if you're offering, I'm going to take you up on it."

I shake my head. This situation with Dixie really has Ward down. *I can relate.* "I'm offering. Come on up. It'll be good to hang out."

My phone beeps. I glance at the screen. Unknown

number. "Hey Ward, I've got to run. Talk later?" I switch callers. "Julian King here."

"Julian, it's Tim Pollard. We met last December?"

I frown. Why is the town councilor calling me? "At the holiday parade." Thank heavens for a working memory. "Hello, Mr. Pollard. How can I help you?"

He clears his throat and sounds embarrassed. "I have a rather large favor to ask. My daughter Elise got engaged last month. She's throwing an engagement party on Saturday, but her caterer just went out of business."

"Ouch."

"Indeed. It's supposed to warm up next weekend. The motels are booked up. Every restaurant in town is bracing for the first flood of tourists. None of them can cover the party in the last minute."

Always say yes to the town council. "I'd be happy to help, if that's where you're going with this."

He exhales in relief. "Thank you so much."

"Not a problem. Sausages aren't exactly elegant..."

He laughs. "Neither is Elise. The party is in Haslem Park at six in the evening. A hundred and fifty guests, if you can believe it."

I definitely need to go shopping. At least the venue's easy. The city put in a community kitchen in Haslem Park last summer. There's a grill, outdoor and indoor ovens, sinks, the works.

"Got it. I'll be there at five to set up."

"Perfect. Oh, I almost forgot to mention. I asked Dakota Wilde to serve pizza too, so you'll have to share the space."

A smile spreads over my face. I find out Dakota thinks I'm hung like a horse, and now this?

Excellent.

This week is off to a flying start.

5

DAKOTA

T his week is crap.

Monday: Saw Julian jog. Julian caught me staring. Bad.

Also Monday: Julian invited me to sleep with him again. For a brief second, until my brain caught up with my idiot libido, I'd seriously considered it.

The real kicker—and yes, still Monday—he heard me say that he was hung like a horse.

After that spectacularly poo-filled start, the week should pick up, right?

Spoiler: It does not.

Tuesday, I don't run into Julian, but he's the main topic of conversation at Daily Grind. "I ran into Beth Shepperd last night," Mildred Bower says to Sally McKee as they both wait in line. "She said that Julian King wants to buy her business." She looks around and lowers her voice. "Did you know Roger Wexler had made her an offer? One hundred and fifty thousand."

"No." Sally draws herself up, an outraged look on her face. "He didn't."

Mildred has a carrying sort of voice. The Daily Grind isn't large. Everyone in the shop is listening to this conversation. Me included.

Mildred nods earnestly. "He told her the place needed to be fixed up. Told her she wouldn't get a better price."

Sally McKee doesn't like Roger Wexler any more than I do. Her lips tighten. "Why didn't Beth talk to someone?"

"You know Beth," Mildred replies. She shuffles forward and orders a green tea. "She doesn't like asking for help." She moves closer to Sally, and finally remembers to lower her voice. "The city fined her for not mowing her lawn."

"What?" This time, it's Sally's voice that fills the shop. "It's the end of April. Everyone's grass looks like a mess." She shakes her head, her expression grim.

She's thinking what I'm thinking. There's really only one conclusion anyone can draw, and that is the obvious one. Roger Wexler is abusing the power of his office, fining Mrs. Shepperd for all kinds of frivolous things, so that he can drain her of money and force her to sell to him.

And Julian's just prevented that from happening. He's a fucking hero.

Sure enough, that's exactly what Mildred says next. "That Julian King. Such a nice young man. I called to order some sausages for our barbecue, and he wouldn't take money for it. And do you know, he's putting in a wheelchair ramp at The Frozen Spoon tomorrow?"

Gah.

I hate myself for it, but on Wednesday, I actually drive by the Frozen Spoon. Sure enough, Mildred was right. Julian is there, in all his shirtless splendor, muscles flexing as he cuts boards with a power saw.

I'm ashamed to admit I ogle. I drive by once, twice, three times. I stare at the raw masculine perfection on display, and then, like a little chickenshit, I run away before Julian can realize I'm checking him out.

Anytime you want the king again, sweetness, you just have to ask.

The real kicker comes Thursday. Tim Pollard calls me. "Dakota, I almost forgot to tell you. I felt terrible about asking you to cater Elise's party when you're an invited guest and a friend of the family, but..."

"It's no problem, Tim," I interrupt. "You know that."

"Yes, still. I asked Julian King if he'd cater as well, and he said he was happy to. Good guy, Julian. He'll be bringing sausages. This way, you won't have to make food for all hundred and fifty guests. Just half of them."

I stare at my phone in shock and horror. "You asked Julian King to cater Elise's party?"

Tim completely misreads my tone. "Yes, I thought you'd be relieved. See you on Saturday, Dakota. And thank you again."

I will be catering Elise's engagement party—a party that both my mother and my brother will be attending—along with Julian King.

Sandra Flanigan's eagle eyes will be on me.

Dom has twin radar. He probably also knows I slept with Julian last year.

In Madison, Julian King, a single, eligible man, is something of a unicorn.

My mother has babies on the brain. Dom and Cat have a wedding Pinterest board. They'll be watching me. Watching my reaction to Julian.

I'll have to pretend I don't want to strangle him. I'll have to pretend that he has no effect on me. I'm going to have to be on my best behavior.

This has disaster written all over it.

JULIAN'S already at Haslem Park when I get there. I'm wearing a purple and blue floral-patterned dress. Julian's eyes light up. "You look very pretty."

"Thank you." There. See? I can be well-behaved.

He looks almost surprised that I don't have a snappy comeback. "You've got stuff in the truck?"

"I can handle it." I can't really, not in the shoes I'm wearing, but I'm not going to admit that to Julian.

"Don't be ridiculous, Dakota," he says. "I've got this." His lips curl up. "You can flutter your eyelashes and tell me how strong I am."

I roll my eyes. "My hero."

Elise's car pulls up, and she and her fiancé Trey get out. "Dakota," she squeals, throwing her arms around me. "Thank you, thank you, thank you."

I laugh and hug her back. "You look fantastic." She's wearing a pale pink sundress that looks amazing against her dark skin.

"So do you."

Trey grins at his fiancée's exuberance and holds out his hand to Julian. "Trey Jackson."

Julian shakes it. "Julian King. Congratulations on your engagement."

"Thank you for bailing us out like this." He wraps his arm around Elise's waist. "I really appreciate it." He leans forward and lowers his voice. "To be honest, I'm much more excited about pizza and sausages than whatever the hell Minerva was making."

Elise shakes her head, but she has a fond smile on her face. "Can we do anything to help?" she asks the two of us.

I shoo her away. "It's your engagement party. Go enjoy it. We've got this under control."

Once Elise and Trey are safely out of earshot, I turn to Julian. "Do you even know what you're doing, or am I going to have to babysit you all evening?"

His teeth flash in a grin. "And there it is. I thought you'd lost your edge, Dakota. I was beginning to get quite worried." He sets up his station quickly, his movements smooth and practiced. "I spent my gap year working in kitchens in Germany. That's where I learned how to make sausages." He winks at me. "I know how to handle my meat, Wilde."

Huh. I didn't know that about Julian. "And here I thought you decided to make sausages for the jokes."

"The jokes were a strong selling point." He takes a half-step toward me. My heart starts to race at the intent, predatory look in his eyes.

His voice turns intimate, as if we're in my bedroom all over again, and he's unbuttoning my shirt, kissing every bit of skin he uncovers. "Before we're done tonight," he says, each word holding a promise of dark sin and uncontrolled pleasure, "You'll eat my sausage, and you'll admit it was the best you've ever had."

It takes a second for the words to penetrate my lust-addled mind.

The jackass.

He deliberately baited me.

I have provocation. If I wrap my hands around his neck right now and squeeze, there's not a jury in the country that would convict me.

I hear the sound of voices. Tim has arrived, along with my mother, Dom, and Cat.

Strangling Julian King will have to wait.

I turn away from Julian, and count to ten in my head. Then I pull out a ball of already-risen pizza dough from its tray and punch it viciously. Am I imagining his face as I smack the dough around?

Hell, yes. Of course I am.

I DON'T WORK in the kitchen anymore at Dakota's Pizza, not unless Teresa Barbini is on vacation. But that's only in the last three or four years. When I first opened my restaurant, I did most of the cooking. I had to; I didn't have enough money to do anything else.

I'm a little rusty, but I quickly find my rhythm. To my surprise, Julian looks perfectly comfortable in the kitchen. Not only that, but he's clearly catered parties before, because he's prepared. He has a sandwich board with his menu lettered on it. Four kinds of sausage—beef, pork, lamb, and a vegetarian one. He sets up an assortment of toppings. Pickled vegetables, grilled onions, relish, mustard, and two kinds of cheese.

He doesn't run around in panic. He doesn't swear and lose his shit when the grill starts to smoke. He just pulls his sausages off, deals with the problem, and gets back on track.

His competence is, frankly, one hell of a turn-on.

"You've done this before."

"So much surprise," he says dryly. "Yes, of course I've done this before, Dakota. I don't just agree to cater a party for a hundred and fifty people without some understanding of what's involved. I run a stall at the Bainbridge farmer's market every Friday morning." His eyes dance with amusement. "They love my meat."

I have to laugh. "Do you ever stop?"

"Hey, the jokes are there," he says easily. "Somebody's got to take them."

One of Julian's better qualities is that he doesn't pout. If I snark, he snarks back. He doesn't back down; he gives as good as he gets.

But it's always good-natured. He's astonishingly hard to ruffle.

Danger, Will Robinson, danger.

I shake my head, trying to jostle the insanity out of my mind. I can't like Julian King. That way lies trouble.

We banter as we work. I don't even have to pretend; I'm having a good time. In a surprisingly short order of time, I've got my pizzas assembled and ready to go in the oven. Julian's at the grill, frying up sausages, and the smell is making my mouth water.

"Admit it, you want to try a piece." He takes a sausage off the grill and holds it toward me. "Open wide, honey. Don't worry, I'll go slow. I won't shove it down your throat."

Damn it. Now I'm picturing myself on my knees, sucking Julian's cock. Arousal skitters down my spine, and a wave of moisture floods between my legs.

"Don't worry." My voice is sugar sweet. "I'll use my teeth. Biting is encouraged, right?"

His eyes go hot with lust. "Whatever you want," he murmurs.

Stop looking at me like you're going to devour me, damn it. Because you're making me want it. You're making me want you.

I stare up at him, my body prickling with desire. The moment stretches. His eyes are locked on my lips, and I have the strangest feeling he's going to kiss me.

And I need it. My fingers shake. My body drowns in need. I crave him with every fiber of my being.

Julian King is my cocaine.

I shake my head, snapping free of his spell. "Stop. Please."

He immediately takes a step back. Concern fills his face. "I'm sorry. I didn't mean to make you uncomfortable."

I know. *That's part of the problem.* I slide my pizza board into the oven. "We're here to do a job. Let's just cater the damn party, okay?"

Guests are filing in. While we were cooking, Elise, Trey, Tim, my mom, Dom, and Cat have set up long tables, covered them with colorful tablecloths, and filled bowls with chips, popcorn, and peanuts. Daddy Yankee sings Con Calma on the speaker. Kids run around. A handful of teenagers toss around a frisbee.

The sun's out. It's beautifully warm, probably the first really nice day so far this year. It's hard to be grouchy.

"Why don't you go join your friends?" Julian suggests. "You're all set up. It's just about getting pizza in and out of the oven at this stage. I can take care of things here."

"You're not going to accidentally spill a bottle of salt on my pizza or something, are you?"

His lips twitch. "I don't need to sabotage you, Dakota. My food holds up. Elise is your friend. This is her engagement party. You don't need be stuck back here. Go have a good time."

I give him a suspicious glare. "Really? That's so *nice* of you."

"Once again, your surprise touches me. Don't worry. I'll turn back into the devil tomorrow morning."

"Who's the guy?"

Tejal Mehta is Elise's maid of honor. She lives in Toronto, she's a surgeon, and she's gorgeous. She's got long black hair, brown eyes, and when she smiles, it lights up the room.

And she's clearly interested in Julian.

I play dumb. "What guy?"

"The guy at the grill." She ogles discreetly. "He's really hot." She gives me a friendly smile. "You two seemed pretty cozy together. I'm not stepping on your toes, am I?"

"Not even a little. He's fair game."

"Oh good." Her eyes light up. "His logo is so funny, I love it. It's so hard to find a guy with a good sense of humor, you know?"

I don't know how to respond, so I nod. It seems safe.

"I've spent the last fifteen minutes looking up sausage jokes on my phone as an icebreaker," she continues.

Julian would love that. My stomach clenches uncomfortably. I ignore it. I don't want him. There's no reason to get in Tejal's way. "What did you find?"

"A million jokes about how things are the wurst," she says. "The one I liked the best goes like this. Two eggs, a sausage, and a pancake walk into a bar. The bartender says, Sorry, we don't serve breakfast here."

I chuckle weakly. "That's a good one," I agree. Damn it, she's perfect for Julian. He's a hotshot ex-lawyer, she's a doctor. They're both from Toronto. I want to claw her eyes out, and I'm horribly ashamed of myself for my bout of jealousy.

She walks up to talk to him. I turn away, and Dom sits down next to me. "So," he says. "You and Julian King."

"Go away."

He laughs. "Mom sent me to pump you for information. Give me something to distract her with."

"Isn't your wedding enough to distract her? Get her involved. Make her choose the flowers or something."

"She offered to be the wedding planner; Cat accepted gratefully. Neither of us care about the ceremony, and mom's generally pretty low-key." He shakes his head. "At least until Margie shares another round of pictures of that grandchild of hers."

I shouldn't smirk. "She hinted she wanted grandkids, didn't she?"

"Hint? She was as subtle as a battering ram. It's every sibling for themselves, Dakota. I'm throwing you under the bus."

"Jerk." There's no heat in my tone. "There's nothing going on between us. Julian's not my type."

He looks over to the grill. I look over too, and immediately regret it. Julian's laughing at something Tejal's saying. A fist squeezes my heart.

Dom catches the look on my face. A smile curls his lips. "I'll tell her that," he says agreeably. He gets on his feet and pats my head. "It's safe to look now. She's gone."

6

JULIAN

I watch Dakota laugh with her friends. I watch her lean forward, her expression animated, as she tells a story. I watch her dance with a guy who's holding her too close, and I fight the urge to march over and shove him out of the way.

It gets late. The crowd thins. I tidy up, do dishes, and pack my stuff away. Dakota walks toward me, her cheeks flushed and her eyes bright. "Hey Julian."

She's been drinking. She's ever so slightly tipsy. She beams at me, friendly and open, and I smile back, because I'm a sucker for her. "Dakota."

"I drank too much of Cat's beer," she confides, moving closer to me, and tipping her face up. She smells like jasmine and strawberries and sunshine. "That stuff packs a punch."

"Yes, it does, baby." I brush a curl back from her cheek, and tuck it behind her ear, and then I realize what I'm doing, and I stop myself.

She notices the kitchen. "You cleaned up."

"Mmm."

"That's nice of you." She tilts her head up at me again. Her lipstick is long gone. Her lips look soft and kissable, and it takes supreme willpower to hold back. Sure, I could kiss her now, but tomorrow morning, she'd wake up firmly convinced I'm a jerk.

I'm playing the long game here.

"Not really. I did it to win points."

"Points for what?"

I give her a direct look. "What do you think, Dakota?"

She bites her lower lip. "You were flirting with Tejal."

"She was flirting with me," I correct her. "I'm not interested in Tejal."

Her expression turns guarded. "Because she's brown?"

"Because she's not you." You wouldn't believe it by the way I'm tossing all my cards on the table, but I'm normally a good poker player.

She inhales sharply. "I don't believe you."

"About what?"

"About wanting me. It's a clever line."

Who hurt you, baby?

I'm a bit of a bastard. I'm not going to seduce her when she's tipsy, but that's where my good behavior ends. The alcohol has lowered her walls enough that we're having a real conversation, and I'm selfish enough that I'm going to exploit it to get some answers.

"Is it?" I hold her gaze in mine. "Fine. I'll make a deal with you. I thought we had a good time last year. Fuck that; I know we had a good time last year. Then the next time I see you, I get the cold shoulder. Tell me why you don't like me, and I'll back away."

There's real attraction between us; I'm convinced of it. But I can only nudge her so far. At some point, if anything is to happen between us, she'll need to take a step.

"You'll back away?"

"The next move will have to come from you."

"There won't be a next move."

Lawyer trick: Always act confident, even when you have no idea what's going to happen. "You're standing too close to me. You're practically rubbing your boobs in my chest. There'll be a next move."

I hope.

She glares at me, her eyes flashing fire. "You are such a cocky asshole, you know that, Julian?"

"Do we have a deal?"

"Fine." She lifts her chin in the air. "You slept with me under false pretenses."

What the fuck? "I have no idea what you're talking about."

"You told me you were a hotshot lawyer from Toronto."

I frown at her. "No, I didn't."

"Yes, you did."

"No," I repeat. "I did not. I remember everything about that day. Zach introduced me as a hotshot lawyer from Toronto, and I said, not exactly."

"You did say that," she agrees. "I assumed you were being modest about being called a hotshot lawyer."

"I am a lot of things, but I'm not modest. I said 'not exactly' because I'd quit my job earlier that month. Why does it matter if I'm a lawyer or not? You don't strike me as the materialistic type."

"It doesn't matter if you're a lawyer," she snaps. "It matters that you moved to Madison. You were supposed to be a one-night stand. I wasn't supposed to see you again."

I still don't understand. "That's why you froze me out? I wanted to date you. If you didn't want to date me, why didn't you just tell me? I'm a big boy; I've heard the word no before."

She makes a scoffing sound in her throat. "There it is again. You don't want to date me, Julian. You just think you do."

I fold my arms over my chest. "First you think I'm feeding you a line when I tell you I'm interested in you, and now this. Go ahead. This ought to be good. Tell me why you think I don't know my own mind."

"You're living some kind of hipster fantasy," she says. "You quit your big-city job and moved to a small town. No longer part of the rat race. Slower pace of life. Time to stop and smell the roses. All that bullshit. Then we sleep together, and it was good, and you've convinced yourself that you want me. Probably because I know how to cook, and you're picturing me wearing an apron, rolling dough out on a counter or something."

I wasn't thinking that. Not until she said it. I am now though, and in my fantasy, she's not wearing anything under the apron.

"I'm right, aren't I?"

"You're off by a mile. Your theory is not only wrong, but it's also insulting. I was making three hundred and fifty thousand dollars a year when I quit. I don't need my partner to be a glorified housekeeper. If I wanted a housekeeper, I made enough damn money to hire one."

Her chin juts out. "You don't want to be in a relationship, you just think you do. And I don't want to be your experiment."

There's a ring of truth to that last part; she definitely doesn't want to be my experiment. But everything else, she's dead wrong about.

I'm on the verge of an insight here. I just have to keep pushing. "Why don't I want to be in a relationship?"

"How old are you?"

"Thirty-four."

"I'm thirty-two," she replies. "More or less your age. How many serious relationships have you been in?"

I sense a trap. "Define serious relationship," I say cautiously.

She rolls her eyes. "Dating someone exclusively for longer than three months."

Ouch. My answer is not going to help my argument. "One."

"I rest my case."

"There were extenuating circumstances. I was in graduate school, and then I went to work for a law firm. I worked eighty hours a week. I wasn't in a relationship because no normal woman wants to date someone who works that much. There was no point inviting someone to share my life in the last six years, because my life was crap."

Dakota shivers, and I wrap my jacket around her shoulders. It's too big for her, and she's swimming in it, and she's still beautiful and vibrantly alive. "Here's the thing, Julian," she says. "Society cons people into thinking they're not complete unless they're with someone, and so we get sucked in. But the truth is, if either of us really wanted to be in a relationship, it would have happened."

I asked her for an answer. Reading between the lines, I got one. Someone hurt her so badly that she's running afraid.

She doesn't get involved with guys from Madison. Last May, she wouldn't have slept with me had she known I was planning a move to her town.

I want to date Dakota. She's funny. Interesting. I can't

stop thinking about her. But I can't offer her the perfect certainty she wants. Nobody can. Life is messy and unpredictable. People fall out of love. They get sick. They die. Nothing is guaranteed forever.

I made a deal—the next move has to come from Dakota.

Except I now know that it's unlikely to happen.

"Come on," I tell her. "I'll give you a ride home. You can come back tomorrow for your car."

"Thank you."

She looks serious and a little sad, and I want to make her laugh. "More people ate my sausages than your pizza," I tell her smugly. "I almost ran out of food."

It works. She draws herself up. "They did not," she says in outrage. "And if you ran out of food, it's because you didn't bring enough." Her voice turns sweet. "Don't sweat it, Julian. With more experience, I'm sure that even you will eventually get it right."

There we are. Back to familiar ground. Trading insults, throwing barbs. And hey, if I want more, what of it?

Sausage King is in the black. Mrs. Shepperd is going to sell me her restaurant. I'm integrating into the community; I got asked earlier this week to supply serdelki to the Legion fundraiser.

By any measure, I lead a pretty charmed life.

I want Dakota, but like I said, nothing is guaranteed. Nobody gets everything they want.

7

DAKOTA

I lie awake for many hours, Julian's words running through my mind.

I'm not interested in Tejal. She's not you.

I wanted to date you.

The next move will have to come from you.

For a second, I let myself imagine what it would be like to date Julian. For one thing, I'd never be bored. Julian is many things—cocky, arrogant, exasperating as hell—but he's not dull.

You'll fight all the time, Practical-Dakota points out.

The make-up sex will be worth it, the more romantic part of me retorts.

You'll get sucked in too deep, Practical-Dakota says. *You haven't dated anyone in a year, and that was just after one night with Julian King. If you date him, when things fall apart—and make no mistake, they will fall apart—your heart will shatter into a million little pieces.*

Romantic Dakota doesn't have anything to counter that, because it's the truth. Julian King, as tempting as he is, is not worth the risk.

A WEEK GOES BY. I don't run into Julian. On Wednesday, ten days after Elise's engagement party, Ben Watanabe, Madison's best and most reliable contractor, stops by to look at the building I'm buying. "Lots of work here," he says laconically, looking around at the dusty and dated interior.

"I know." The building is in a prime location—right on Front Street—but it's stood vacant for almost ten years as Neil and Anna Silvers, the owners of the building, went through an acrimonious separation, followed by an even more contentious divorce. In an effort to spite their partner, neither of the Silvers did anything to maintain the place. The yard is a weed-filled mess. A couple of the front windows are broken. The floors are water damaged. The drywall is moldy and will need to be replaced. And that's the obvious stuff.

"When do you close?"

"Next month. First week of June."

He nods thoughtfully. "You want to open this year?"

"If possible, yes. I thought that if I could open by the end of July or early August, I'll be able to squeeze a month or two out of the tourist season."

He shakes his head at once. "This will take longer than eight weeks, Dakota."

I thought he'd say that. "I talked to Silver. He knows what a mess this place is. He'll allow the work to get started right away." Neil Silver is not my favorite person. I hadn't wanted to ask him for the favor; I'd had to swallow my pride to make the call. But I couldn't ignore the economics. Dakota's Pizza makes eighty percent of its yearly revenue in four months—June, July, August, and September. If I can't get this expansion done in time, I'll barely be making enough to cover the mortgage.

Ben frowns thoughtfully. "It's unorthodox, but you're not the only one doing it," he says. "King is too. He's got us building a deck in front of Mrs. Shepperd's place this week."

Irritation floods me. Damn it. I was counting on Ben being able to start my job quickly. As soon as I signed on the dotted line, I'd called him and told him to clear his schedule for me. Now Julian's poaching my contractor.

"He does?" My words are coated with ice.

Ben knows me well. "Relax, the deck's a quick job. Two, three days. I wasn't planning to take it on; I even told King I was too busy."

And yet, once again, Julian's getting his own way. "What made you change your mind?"

"Mrs. Shepperd," he says. "King's not taking possession until the start of July. If I can get this deck built, then she can use it until the deal closes." He spreads his hands. "She's pretty hard up for money, Dakota. She could use a couple of good months. I've got to say; I have a lot of respect for King. He could have played hardball with Mrs. Shepperd, but unlike Wexler, he's being a stand-up guy. Really shows you what he's made of."

Gah. Even my contractor loves Julian.

"Can you start next week?"

He pulls out his phone and checks his schedule. "Yes. The job should take ten weeks, give or take. I'll email you a quote tonight. I need a ten percent deposit to hold the spot."

"Not a problem."

Ten weeks. That'll put me at the start of August. Ben's extremely reliable. He always delivers on time and on budget.

My spirits start to rise. I've already applied for a restaurant permit. I have a line of credit secured against Dakota's Pizza; it will allow me to borrow up to two hundred thousand dollars. That should cover the cost of renovation.

Looks like things are on track.

My phone rings. It's Sherri Stephenson. "Dakota," she says, her voice somber. "Are you busy this afternoon? The council would like to talk to you about your restaurant permit."

Anxiety floods me.

Here's the thing. Apart from four years in Queens to get an art history degree I don't use, I've lived in Madison all my life. I know how this town works.

When the council calls you in for a meeting to discuss your new restaurant permit?

It's not good.

It's not good at all.

8

DAKOTA

B y the time the afternoon rolls around, I've worked myself into a tizzy.

Fuck this shit. Just last year, the council—and more specifically Roger Wexler—absolutely dicked over Cat and Vicki. For the space of a day or two, we were petrified they wouldn't get a food permit. Cat, my soon-to-be sister-in-law, had invested all her money in the brewpub. She'd been facing financial ruin.

I'm not in the best mood when I arrive at the town hall Wednesday afternoon. My mood does not improve when I see Julian there. My stupid heart starts to beat faster, and my throat goes dry, and fool that I am, I still want him. "What are you doing here?" I snap. "Taking up stalking in your spare time?"

I regret biting his head off the second the words leave my mouth. I'm about to apologize when his face settles into a mask. "Stalking you?" he says, his voice clipped. "Don't flatter yourself, Dakota. As you've said, it wasn't that memorable."

For a second, I forget to breathe. Pain slashes through

me, like salt robbed into a cut that's has never quite healed. First a second, all thought flees my mind, and all that is left is raw, visceral emotion.

Regret flashes across Julian's face. "Dakota," he starts. "I didn't mean..."

The door opens, and Sherri stands in the doorway, looking from Julian to me with an intrigued expression on her face. More fodder to the gossip mill. "The Council is ready for you," she says.

I straighten my shoulders. The last man I let hurt me was my father, and that was twenty years ago. I will not let Julian affect me. I refuse to give him the satisfaction. Ignoring him completely, I walk into the meeting room.

All five councilors are seated around the oval conference table. Roger Wexler is at the head of the table, wearing his trademark oily smile. Tim Pollard sits at his right, flipping through the binder in front of him. He looks up when we enter and smiles warmly at both of us.

Mina Ahuja's seated next to Tim. Across from Mina, Sally McKee is in a low-voiced conversation with Jeffrey Shun.

The full council for a routine restaurant permit. *Trouble.*

Sherri sits back down in her chair, giving me a small, sympathetic smile. *Definitely trouble.* Sherri knows everything that happens in town. If she's offering up sympathy, then I'm really not going to like what's about to happen.

I shove the hurt I felt at Julian's words to the backburner; it's not important. Right now, I have bigger fish to fry.

There are two open seats around the table, directly across from each other. I walk to one and sit down. Julian settles in the other. I look around the room, ignoring the way Julian dwarfs the chair. He's wearing a charcoal grey suit today, one that hugs his broad shoulders. Julian King would look good wearing a torn shirt and cut-off shorts, but there's something very sexy about a man in a well-tailored suit. It's probably because he radiates confidence from every pore.

Stop thinking about Julian.

There are three other people—two men and a woman—that I don't recognize. Sally briskly performs introductions. "Marvin Hale, manager of the Bainbridge location of The Friendly Crown. Don Mazzio of We Knead Pizza. Valentina Greyson of La Mesa. Julian King, the owner of Sausage King. Dakota Wilde, the owner of Dakota's Pizza."

Well, crap. Julian and I are the only small business owners here. The Friendly Crown is a chain, as is We Knead Pizzeria, and La Mesa. The big guys are sniffing around our little town, and that's not good. We get a lot of tourists in the summer, but still. The chains have deep pockets. They can afford to undercut us, take a loss for a year or two, and drive us out of business.

Last year, Roger Wexler had been all gung-ho about making sure chain restaurants didn't invade Madison. Less than a year later, three of them are here for a permit? This stinks to high heaven.

I look around at the councilors. "I'm not quite clear what this meeting is about," I begin. There you go. That's nice and non-confrontational.

Jeffrey Shen looks up. "The five of you have all applied for restaurant permits," he says. "Normally, permit approvals are routine business. However, five new restaurants are a lot in a town our size."

Tell me about it. "We used to have three grocery stores in town," Mr. Shun continues. "Two of them have shut down, and in their place, there's a gift shop selling T-shirts and magnets and other assorted junk, and there is a sports bar.

What is worse—neither of these businesses are open year-round, just for tourist season."

I don't know where he's going with this. I nod to cover my confusion.

"The council is very concerned," Tim chimes in. "Madison is rapidly turning into a town where every business caters to tourists, and nothing caters to our tax-paying residents. We used to have a pharmacy, but it's closed now. If you want to buy clothes, you have to drive to the nearest large city. Garden center? We don't have one. No gyms. No dentists. No daycares. Instead, what we have are gift shops, bars, and restaurants."

"Previous councilors have prioritized tourism over the needs of Madison's residents," Sally McKee says. "It's gone too far. We're asking our seniors to drive two hours to get their prescription filled. That's not acceptable."

Damn it, they're going to deny my permit. I grit my teeth in frustration. Yes, I agree with the overall principle of what Sally is saying. The town council has allowed unbridled development for more than twenty years, and yes, it's not a healthy dynamic. Year after year, people move away from Madison because the only jobs you can find here are seasonal. The more people go away, the less the need for essential services. It's a vicious cycle, and every year, it seems to get a little worse.

All the same, there's a part of me that wants to bang my head repeatedly on the desk in front of me. Why me? I bought the empty building next to Dakota's pizza, assuming the restaurant permit was a formality. I'm fifty thousand dollars in the hole, and that's not counting the ten-percent deposit I verbally promised Ben Watanabe. Why has the town council picked the worst time in the world to rethink its policy?

Julian leans forward. "I can't disagree with anything you've said," he says, his voice calm and reasonable. "However, if I might respectfully remind the council, tourism is the biggest source of revenue in Madison. Tourists pour money into our economy, money that benefits our residents. Last September, there was a forty-five-minute line outside Dakota's Pizza almost every day. The Madison Brewpub is similarly busy, as is every other restaurant in town. If we can't cater to their needs, the tourists will go elsewhere. Surely, preserving our biggest source of revenue is a priority."

As much as I hate to admit it, Julian's good. His argument is measured and logical, and it might work.

Mina Ahuja nods in agreement. "That's exactly what I said."

Roger Wexler speaks up for the first time. "We already voted," he reminds Mina. "We're only going to grant one permit application this year." He looks around at us. "The five of you are all qualified. Selecting one of you would be arbitrary, and we don't want to do that. We weren't sure how to resolve the impasse, and then Sally had an idea."

Sally leans forward, her eyes sparkling with enthusiasm. "A reality-style contest," she announces triumphantly. "In an outdoor tent. No swearing, no fighting. Everyone plays nice. For three weeks this summer, you'll compete against each other, and at the end of it, we'll crown a winner."

"The winner will get the restaurant permit," Roger Wexler adds.

Yeah, that part was perfectly obvious, Roger.

I stare at Sally. She's normally a rational person, but right now, she's practically falling out of her chair in excitement. "You want to do the Great British Bake Off. In Madison. With the five of us." Is she crazy? Summer's almost here. The tourists will soon be swarming us in relentless waves. We don't have time for games.

"Exactly," she beams. "I just love that show. Everyone so nice to each other. So friendly, so collaborative. Do you know, when one of them got married, the other contestants all attended the wedding, and even made wedding cakes for the bride and groom?"

Heaven help me, we have a GBBO groupie.

"It'll be great for tourism," Mina says. "There's a new hotel in Barrel Beach. A developer is building a resort in Marmet. We can't take the tourists for granted; we have to work hard at entertaining them."

Tim nods. "Rana will publicize the contest. She'll arrange for a crew to film it, and we're going to put it on the internet. She's already talked to TVO. They've agreed to put it on their website to give us a publicity boost. They might even air it on TV."

Great. Just great. Rana Halabi is Madison's new social media manager. She's twenty-five. She's relentlessly enthusiastic, smart as a whip, and is determined to pull Madison into the digital age. She started in March, and in two short months, she's got the entire council eating out of her hand. If Rana's behind this, we're doomed.

I contemplate my options. If I don't get this permit, I'd lose my deposit, all fifty thousand dollars. I cannot afford that.

As much as I want to tell the council to fuck off, it's not really an option.

Then again, neither is participating in a stupid reality contest at the height of the tourist season.

I have to try to ward this off. "We're busy during summer. As Julian pointed out, Dakota's Pizza has a line out the door. None of us have time for this."

Across the room, Julian smiles at me, a challenging gleam in his eyes. "On the contrary," he says. "Count me in. Dakota might not be able to pull this off, but I'm game. I'll be happy to put my food up against anyone." He turns to me, a wicked smile dancing on his lips. "I guarantee it'll measure up."

Ha ha. Everybody's a comedian.

I lift my chin in the air. *You want a challenge, buddy? I'll give you a challenge.* "Fine, I'm in too."

Pleasure surges through me at the thought of beating Julian King for the last restaurant permit.

Bring it on, wiener boy.

9

JULIAN

Goddammit, I don't want to be in competition with Dakota. If it wasn't for the three other people there, I'd just walk away from the whole fucking mess. I'm not a puppet to dance to the bidding of the asshole town council.

It wasn't that memorable? What the hell were you thinking, King?

That's just it. I wasn't thinking. She walked in, her silky blouse caressing her pert, perky breasts, a tight pencil skirt hugging her round ass, her hair hanging in soft waves around her face, and all the blood left my brain.

I drag my attention back to the room. Now that the councilors have the five of us on board their insane scheme, they're all smiles. "I'll get Rana," Sally McKee says brightly. "She can go over the rules."

She gets up and lets a dark-haired young woman into the room. She looks really familiar. I'm trying to figure out where I know her from when Sally does introductions. "Everyone, this is Rana Halabi," she says. "Rana is Madison's social media manager. She'll be your point person for this contest. Rana, can you go over the rules?"

Ah. She's Yossef Halabi's daughter. I haven't seen her in years. She's all grown up.

"Absolutely." Rana smiles around at the room. "Hello, everyone. The rules are pretty straightforward. On three Saturdays in May and June, we're running an outdoor fair in Haslem Park. There will be rides, a band, beer tents, the works. And of course, you will provide the food."

Of course. This way, they don't even have to contract us for vendor services.

"There will be three rounds," Rana continues. "The first two weeks, the person with the lowest sales will be eliminated. On the third week, the last three contestants will compete in a final." She looks around. "Any questions?"

Dakota raises her hand. "What prevents the chains from underpricing their food to sell more?" she asks, glaring at the guy from We Knead Pizza.

"We've considered that," Rana replies. "For each event, you will be given a budget. You must buy your food at retail price; we will audit your numbers to ensure that there's no cheating. And the winner will be the person that both hits a threshold of unit sales and makes the most money." She hands around a set of folders. "Full details are in the binders."

There are a couple of more questions from the others. I flip through the folder as I listen. Rana's thought of everything—no surprise there, Yossef is one of the most detail-oriented lawyers I know.

"If that's all, then I'll see you on the Friday of Victoria Day weekend at six in the evening in Haslem Park. The dates are in your binders. I'll audit your food and budget, and as soon as I'm done, you'll be given four hours to do any prep you need."

The meeting breaks up. Rana approaches me with a smile on her face. "Julian," she says, giving me a friendly hug. "I thought it was you."

"Hey, Rana." I return her hug and over her shoulder, Dakota gives me a death glare.

Hang on. She's jealous?

Oh, this is hilarious. I've been friends with Youssef for a good ten years now. Rana will always be the painfully shy kid with pigtails.

But Dakota doesn't know that. My smile widens. I'm going to milk this situation for all it's worth. "I haven't seen you since you left for college. How've you been, kid?"

"Good." She looks up at me, her eyes twinkling. "My dad is still pissed you quit."

I laugh. Youssef Halabi is a partner at BCF, and a mentor of mine. He'd been extremely vocal about his feelings when I told him of my plans to resign. "Trust me, I know. He called me into his office and chewed me out for an hour."

"That sounds like him," she agrees. "You've been doing this for a year, then? It's going well?"

"I can't complain," I tell her. "Tell me about you. You're Madison's social media manager? When did this happen? And why?"

"I've been doing it remotely for the last few months," she replies. "I only moved into Madison in March. My boyfriend lives in Marmet, and I wanted to be closer to him."

"You've been here two months and you haven't looked me up? I'm offended."

"I didn't know it was you," she exclaims. "I knew you'd quit BCF, but I had no idea you were making sausages. I only learned last week that you were the guy behind

Sausage King." She grins. "Great name, by the way. And I love the logo."

The logo is a sausage with a cheeky expression on his face and a crown on his head. Everyone who sees it laughs. It's funny and memorable, and it's probably responsible for a good quarter of my business.

"Thank you." Dakota's nowhere in sight. I need to catch up with her and apologize for snapping at her earlier. "Listen, I've got to run. Call me. We'll grab a drink and catch up."

DAKOTA'S TALKING to Tim Pollard in the town hall's lobby. I wait for her to finish her conversation, and then fall into step with her.

She frowns at me. "What do you want, Julian?" she snaps.

"To apologize. I shouldn't have said what I did. Apart from the fact that it was unforgivably rude, it's also not true."

For a fraction of a second, her expression softens. Then she's back to cranky. "Sure," she scoffs. "I'm so memorable, and yet you're hugging every single woman in a fifty-kilometer radius."

I want to pump my fist in the air in celebration. "Jealous, Wilde?"

"I feel sorry for Rana," she replies loftily. "Does she know what she's getting into? The incessant sausage puns are the *wurst*."

I grin. "Did you just make a sausage pun, Wilde? Wurst is a little obvious, but I'll give you marks for effort." I give her a sidelong look. "You have nothing to be jealous about. Rana's father is an old friend."

"Once again, I'm not jealous," she retorts. "You make nice to the person running the contest, King. You're going to need all the help you can get to avoid elimination in the first round. You're out of your league, buddy. You're just a guy with some fancy meat, and everyone else is an experienced restaurateur."

"Fancy meat." I wink at her. "Another compliment. You flatter me, Wilde." An idea strikes me. "Tell you what. You're so sure I'm going to get eliminated? Bet on it."

She turns to me, her blue eyes intrigued. "A bet? What will I get if I win?"

She's biting. "What do you want?"

Her gaze turns speculative. "You'll cook in my kitchen for a week," she says finally.

"Do your bidding for a week?"

"Scared, King?"

I like it when she calls me King. "Intrigued. You're on. But if I don't get eliminated in the first round, I win our bet. And I want..."

She waits for me to continue.

"I find myself with a very particular fantasy," I murmur. "If I win, you'll cook for me. In my kitchen. Naked, wearing nothing but an apron. And you'll eat with me, still naked. Appetizer, entree..." My voice lowers. "And dessert."

Her eyes go wide. Her breath catches. "I thought you said you'd back off."

"You don't have to take the bet, Wilde. Nobody's twisting your hand. You can just walk away."

Say yes, Dakota. Come on. Take one small step toward me.

Her chin lifts. "And lose out on a week of free labor? I don't think so. Fine. You're on, King."

Yes! "I'll be thinking of you tonight." My voice is low. She steps closer. "I'm going to lie in my bed and picture you in that apron and nothing else."

She tilts her head up and parts her lips. Her voice is a breathless whisper. "You are?"

"Mm-hmm." I have her exactly where I want her. "I'll be thinking of you when I touch myself, my darling bratwurst."

Outrage wars with laughter in her eyes. Laughter wins. "My darling bratwurst? That's what you're going with?"

Her face lights up when she smiles. "It was either that or 'sweet relish.'"

"Jackass." She looks around and lowers her voice. "I'm going to masturbate tonight too," she murmurs.

My cock turns rock hard. "You are?" I stare at her, making no effort to hide my need.

"Yes, Julian," she whispers. "I'm going to close my eyes, and I'm going to imagine you beating your schnitzel."

Beating my schnitzel.

"You do realize that making schnitzel involves..."

"Taking a piece of meat and hammering it with a mallet until it's paper thin?" Her smile is vicious. "Oh yes, Julian. I absolutely do. That's exactly what I'm going to be fantasizing about." She stands up on tiptoe and brushes a kiss over my cheek. "Sleep well tonight, King. I know I will."

DAKOTA

You know what I hate about Julian?

He's funny.

On any other guy, the cocky master-of-the-universe act would be seriously annoying. But Julian doesn't take himself seriously. He says the most outrageous things with a twinkle in his eye.

My darling bratwurst.

I start to giggle as I walk back to Dakota's Pizza. When I left town hall, I'd been fuming at their high-handed actions. Now, I can't stop laughing. *It was either that or 'sweet relish.'*

He's a dangerous guy, Julian King.

LATER THAT NIGHT, I get back home, shower and change into my sleep shorts and a tank top. I walk into the kitchen and pour myself a glass of wine.

And my thoughts boomerang back to Julian, back to that first night. Back to when things had been so much simpler.

I settle on my couch and set the glass next to me. The

memories from that fateful day flood my mind, one after the other.

I'd noticed him as soon as I'd walked into the Madison Brewpub. He was sitting with Zach and Penny and some of their friends. He'd been wearing a white shirt, the sleeves rolled up to his elbows. His hair was dark and slightly mussed. He had a tattoo on his forearm. From where I stood, it looked like a quote of some sort, but I couldn't read it.

He was gorgeous, but that's not the reason I looked twice.

No. It was the confidence. He leaned back in his chair, a beer in front of him, and a lazy smile playing about on his lips. Then Zach said something, and his smile widened. The dimple on his chin deepened.

Then he'd lifted his eyes up, as if he'd felt the weight of my stare. Our gazes had locked.

For a second, the pub had disappeared. The noise had faded away. The rest of the crowd receded to the background, and the only person that mattered was the hot stranger staring at me.

Zach had seen me, waved me over. I'd squeezed in next to the guy. "Hi," he'd said, not waiting for Zach to introduce us. "I'm Julian King."

"Dakota Wilde."

Zach had introduced me to the rest of his friends. "Julian's my hotshot lawyer," he'd finished.

Julian's smile had widened. "Not exactly." He'd turned to me, and my breathing had faltered under the effect of that smile. "Dakota," he'd said, his voice a low, intimate murmur. "Can I buy you a beer?"

It hadn't been the most original of pick-up lines. It hadn't mattered. He'd said my name and my heart had almost jumped out of my chest.

We'd talked for a little while. Nothing important, nothing personal. Those were my rules.

Every time Julian asked me a question about myself, I'd deflected it. Did Julian catch what I was doing? Probably. Julian isn't stupid.

That night though, it hadn't been about communication, or feelings, or emotions.

It had been about sex. Raw, carnal, sex.

Had it really? You could have gone to his hotel room. Instead, you brought him back here. To your house. You slept with him in your bedroom.

I push that inconvenient voice away and take a gigantic gulp of my wine.

He'd sat down on this very couch. "Come here," he'd said, his voice low and intent, his hot eyes not attempting to disguise his lust.

He'd pulled me down on his lap. Threaded his hands through my hair and pulled me close. His chocolate brown eyes had locked on mine. "Dakota."

"Julian," I'd whispered. "Are you going to kiss me?"

He'd run his thumb over my lower lip. I'd sucked his finger into my mouth, and his eyes had turned hooded. "Dakota," he'd said. "I'm going to do a whole lot more than that."

His lips had crashed into mine.

I slide my hand down my shorts, thinking about the way Julian's hand had squeezed my throbbing breasts. My insides tighten. My nipples are swollen, erect, aching. He'd sucked them between his teeth. "How hard do you like it?" he'd asked, his eyes promising wicked sin.

"Keep going," I'd replied, throwing my head back and letting my body dance at the knife edge of pleasure and pain.

"So fucking sexy." He'd watched the desire wash over my face. Watched the way I bit my lip. A smile had flickered over his lips as I'd hissed. "Too hard, Dakota?"

"Keep going," I'd said again.

I'm soaked. My body remembers Julian King, and it wants more. My pussy is slick. My fingers find my clit, and I circle the tight bud.

My nipples had throbbed the next day. I'd felt it every time I moved, and I'd savored the twinge of pain. It helped me remember the most incredible night of my life.

He'd gone down on his knees. Right here. He'd spread my thighs apart. Yanked my panties aside. He'd stopped then, and his eyes had feasted me in. "So fucking pretty," he'd murmured. "You're gorgeous, Dakota."

A shiver wracks my body. My insides are heavy with need. I pinch my nipples, close my eyes and imagine Julian next to me, his teeth white against my skin, nipping my tender peaks. "Still harder, naughty girl?"

"Keep going," I'd clenched out for the third time.

He'd laughed then. He pulled me close and kissed me deep. "You're fearless, aren't you?" he'd whispered against my lips. "You're driving me crazy."

I'm not fearless. I'm the biggest coward in the world. But sore nipples heal easier than a broken heart.

He'd thrust his fingers deep into me, his clever tongue still toying with my clit, and that had been the final push I'd needed. I'd exploded, shaking, writhing, my climax washing over me in relentless waves.

He'd sat back up on the couch. "Get back here," he'd ordered, patting his lap. His bulge had been clearly visible underneath his pants. I'd run my palm over it, and he'd thrown his head back, pleasure etched on his face. "Fuck me, that feels good."

I work my clit, Julian's remembered voice whispering encouragement in my ears. "Come for me, baby," he'd murmured as he'd worked me over yet again. I'd been on his lap, grinding my ass on his cock. He wouldn't let me close my eyes. "You want this orgasm? Look at me. Keep your eyes open."

The moment had been intimate, far too intimate for a one-night stand. I should have ignored his words. I should have closed my eyes and hidden from him.

But I wanted it too. The thought of being that vulnerable should have made me flinch away, but I'd wanted him to see me fall apart.

So, I had. I'd looked into his eyes, and I'd let myself shatter.

Is Julian doing this now, in his cottage? Is he sitting on his couch too, or is he lying in bed, fisting his thick, fat cock? Is he thinking of me, the way I'm thinking of him?

Or is he picturing schnitzel? Is he picturing me pounding a piece of meat with a mallet, and wincing at the mental image? Has he dismissed me as someone who's not worth the hassle?

Vicki doesn't understand why I'm mean to Julian. I'm not sure I can articulate it either. The snark is protection. I need it to survive.

He'd rolled a condom on. Right here, on this couch. He'd loomed over me. Taken his cock in his hand and teased my opening. "You want this?"

"Yes," I'd breathed. "Please."

"Good," he'd replied. Then he'd thrust into me, hard and deep. His fingers had dug into my hips. I'd braced myself, one leg on the floor, another on the couch, every nerve in my body coming alive as he pounded me, relentless, driven, powerful.

My insides twist and coil. My toes brace against my rug as I shudder, right there on the edge. I picture Julian, his eyes closed, his hand stroking his throbbing cock. And it's that image that pushes me over. My climax rips through me, and it leaves me limp and drained.

But not sated. For that, I need Julian.

Is that why you took his bet, Dakota? You're hoping he won't be eliminated, and you'll be forced to cook him dinner naked except for an apron. You want Julian again, but you won't admit it. You want to be backed into a corner. You want him to win.

Ugh. I drain the rest of my wine, but this time, it doesn't shut down my inner voice. It mocks me all night long, delivering uncomfortable truths, telling me things I'm not ready to hear.

11

JULIAN

Of course, I masturbate that night. Not even the schnitzel imagery is enough to quell my hard-on. I lie in bed and close my eyes, and I imagine Dakota, wearing an apron and nothing else. She's holding a can of whipped cream, and her eyes are hot with lust.

Her gaze drops to my erection, and then she gets down on her knees. "Let me take care of that for you," she purrs.

Then she sprays the whipped cream on my dick.

Fuck me, my imagination is good. I almost come from that visual.

Back to the fantasy.

Dakota looks up at me, her lips curling into a wickedly sexy smile. "Dessert is my favorite part of the meal." She takes me deep into her mouth, her pretty little lips wrapped around my length, her eyes fixed on me.

Oh fuck.

I throw my head back and groan. My hand fists my cock as my fantasies run rampant. Dakota's pretty pink tongue licking whipped cream off my cock. Her brilliant blue eyes, dazed with desire. Her tight little pussy, slick with arousal.

My hand moves faster and faster, and then I erupt with a muffled shout.

God, I have it bad for her.

I GET up to clean the mess, and then sink back into bed.

I'm going to close my eyes, and I'm going to imagine you beating your schnitzel.

I can't bite back my grin. *Schnitzel.* Her eyes had gleamed wickedly when she told me she'd be masturbating to images of my cock being pounded with a mallet.

Maddening woman.

Then again, she didn't back away from the bet. I told her exactly what I wanted. To be perfectly honest, I'd expected her to run. After all, she's run every other time.

But this time, she hadn't.

She'd stood her ground, lifted that stubborn chin in the air, and told me that she was in.

Yes!

I talked to Ward over the weekend. "What's so special about this girl?" he'd asked. "I don't think I've ever seen you chase someone."

He's right; I haven't. I've never looked for something serious. There were always plenty of women in Toronto who were just as busy with their own careers, who were looking for exactly what I was. An uncomplicated hookup, and nothing more.

I've never thrown myself at a woman this way before. Sometimes, I ask myself if it's worth it.

The answer is always yes.

Three years ago, I'd run my first marathon on a whim. I had a sedentary job, and once I hit my thirties, I was starting to feel out of shape. So, I set a goal.

At first, getting up in the morning to go for a run, especially in winter, was excruciating. I would do all kinds of things to keep myself motivated. Set up fun playlists, put my shoes right by the door, you name it, I did it. Yet every morning, when the alarm went off, I'd lie in bed and ask myself if the run was worth it.

The moment my feet hit the curb, the moment the crisp, cold dawn air slapped my face, I had my answer.

Dakota is like that early morning run.

I put myself out there, over and over again, and I keep getting shot down.

I tell her I want to date her; she tells me I don't know my own mind. I make the most outrageous sausage jokes to get a reaction from her, and she responds with snark. Don't get me wrong, the snark is hilarious, and I love that Dakota can give back as good as she gets. Somebody who agrees with me all the time would bore me to tears.

But—and trust me, I'm well aware of how pathetic I sound—I wish I knew where I stood with her.

This time, she hadn't said no.

Now all I have to do is make sure that I don't fuck up.

I SPENT most of Thursday morning making sausages. In the afternoon, once I'm done, I clean up, take a quick shower, and head over to The Frozen Spoon to see how Ben Watanabe is making out.

Ben and two of his crew members are already there when I arrive. "King," Ben greets me. "I thought I might run into you here."

Yeah, yeah, I'm a control freak. "I dropped by to see how you're making out."

"I'm fine," Ben says. He jerks his head toward the building. "Mrs. Shepperd, on the other hand..." His voice trails away.

I have a strange memory. I don't remember names very well, but numbers stick in my head. Today is the one-year anniversary of the day Jim Shepperd died.

That's why she's upset.

I suppress a groan. I don't want to talk to Beth Shepperd. I never know what to say in these situations. Empathy isn't really my thing. Someone like Dakota would know exactly what to say to comfort Mrs. Shepperd. Me? I'm about as useful as a lump of cheese.

She has friends in Madison, I tell myself. I shift my feet uncomfortably and avoid making eye contact with Watanabe. "Yeah," I mutter. "It's the day her husband died."

He frowns. "It is? I didn't realize that. But that's not why she's upset. She got some new notice from the city. They're harassing her again."

For one brief second, I contemplate not getting involved.

Mrs. Shepperd still hasn't committed to selling her restaurant to me. The wheelchair ramp wasn't expensive to install, but the deck is going to cost between ten and fifteen thousand dollars. The permit cost another five hundred, not to mention the aggravation of having to participate in a reality TV contest because of it.

I'm getting sucked in, deeper and deeper, committing both time and money to The Frozen Spoon, all of it on the assumption that Mrs. Shepperd is going to sign on the dotted line.

But she hasn't signed yet.

Pressure from the city will work to my advantage. It is in my best interest to do nothing and let Mrs. Shepperd fight her own battles.

Julian, you're robbing an old lady, Ward's disapproving voice rings in my ears.

I shrug that aside; I've a lot of experience ignoring Ward.

Then I picture Dakota's face. I imagine her look of contempt when she realizes that I could've helped, but instead chose to do nothing.

Damn it.

Biting back a curse, I make my way up the ramp and knock on the door. After a couple of minutes, it opens. "Julian," Beth Shepperd says, her voice flat and drained of life. "What can I do for you?"

"Ben told me you got a notice from the city."

She sighs. "It's more of Wexler's harassment," she says, sounding defeated.

What is it this time? It can't be the lawn: I mowed it after I installed the wheelchair ramp. "What's going on?"

"Sherri told me I needed to get my restaurant permit modified to include the deck," she says. "Jim always took care of stuff like that. I was nervous about it, but Sherri helped me fill out the form, and she told me it was routine."

"They denied it?"

She nods. "Yes, they did. I got the notice today."

The pulse of anger takes me by surprise. "Can I see it?"

"If you'd like." She disappears inside and returns with a piece of paper. I scan it. The note from the city is brief and is signed by Roger Wexler.

It rejects Mrs. Shepperd's permit modification. "You may not use the deck as additional seating," he writes, the odious fucker. "If we find that food or drink is being consumed on the deck, please note that you will be fined."

My temper flares. "It's outside," Mrs. Shepperd says, her voice hopeless. "On a nice sunny day, how am I supposed to stop people from hanging out on the deck?"

She'll have to block it off. Customers will grumble. Mrs. Shepperd will be caught between a rock and a hard place.

Her eyes fill with tears. "Jim was always going to put a deck," she says. "He handled the paperwork. He would've known what to do. I should know more about my business, I know, but the truth is, all I ever wanted to do was make ice cream. He took care of the business stuff, and I got to experiment." She wipes her eyes with the back of her hand. "A year later, and I miss him every day."

I can't do a damn thing about her pain. The city, on the other hand, is a problem I can help her with. "Jim was going to build a deck?"

"Two years back. He even got a building permit."

"Why didn't he build it?"

"He was a contractor. He got busy with another job. You know what they say. The shoemaker's kids go without shoes."

While The Frozen Spoon never made much money, from all accounts, it ran like a well-oiled machine when Jim Shepperd was alive. Mr. and Mrs. Shepperd really did have a perfect partnership. She made delicious ice-cream, and he took care of everything else.

I follow a hunch. "Do you have a copy of the deck permit? Can I see his paperwork?

Her eyebrow arises. "Sure," she says. "Come on in. Jim filed everything. It's probably still in the office."

I follow her into the room and stop dead in my tracks. Evidently, neither Jim nor Beth Shepperd believed in throwing anything away. There are three shoulder-high filing cabinets in the office. This is going to be like looking for a needle in a haystack.

I start opening drawers at random and rifling through files. It's not as bad as it looks. Jim Shepperd saved everything, but he was methodical. Less than twenty minutes of searching, and I hit pay dirt.

Mrs. Shepperd is in the kitchen. I knock on the open door. "Your restaurant permit already covers the deck," I tell her. "Your husband filed an extension with the city and got approval the year he was planning to build the deck. The city sends you a renewal notice every year, and you've been paying it. You don't need a new permit."

She looks confused. "Wouldn't the city have known that?"

I nod grimly. "They should have," I reply. "They should have searched through the records when they received your application."

Except Roger Wexler is still furious that Mrs. Shepperd turned down his offer. I know what this is. This is a petty act of spite. This is corruption, pure and simple, and this is bullying.

No matter how cynical lawyers are, and trust me, we're cynical bunch, every lawyer I've met—including myself—went into the profession in order to make a difference. To make the world a better place, to see that justice was upheld.

Wexler's harassment of Mrs. Shepperd is flagrant injustice, and I'd be damned if I'm going to sit by and watch him get away with it.

"Mrs. Shepperd, would you be interested in hiring me as your attorney?"

She gives me a puzzled look. "I thought you were retired."

"I quit my job, but I'm still a member of the Ontario Law Society," I reply absently, thinking about next steps. "I'm still licensed." I'm a litigator. I have to do some research before I draft my reply to the city of Madison. Probably get on the phone and talk to some of my ex-colleagues who have more experience dealing with this kind of matter.

"I can't afford you."

I nod toward her display. "I'll take a cone of that ginger rhubarb as a retainer."

She gives me a very peculiar look. "Julian King," she says. "Wouldn't it make more sense for you not to help me?"

"Probably."

"Then why are you helping me? Out of the goodness of your heart?"

I laugh shortly. "I'm an ex-lawyer, Mrs. Shepperd. We don't have hearts. Wexler's bullying you. I loathe bullies."

She gives me another curious look. "Thank you for your help," she says. She goes behind the freezer and reaches for a cup. I shake my head at once. "Sugar cone, please."

She laughs. "Candace was the same way," she says, referring to my dead grandmother. "She would come in every week in the summer. Always asked for a sugar cone." She smiles at me. "She liked the ginger rhubarb too."

"I know. She always had some in her freezer when I visited."

As a kid, I lived for July and August, for lazy swims in the lake, my grandfather's smoked beef brisket, my grandmother's potato salad, all the pie and ice-cream I could eat, and above all, for the abundance of love and affection my grandparents showered me with.

All my life, my grandmother was the only person who didn't automatically assume I'd become a lawyer like my parents. She was the only one who encouraged me to follow my dreams. She left me the cottage in her will.

She died last March. I miss her every day.

I tuck the notice in my back pocket, take the ice cream

cone Mrs. Shepperd hands me, and head back up the driveway, waving goodbye to Ben Watanabe.

Dakota walks by as I reach the street. She stops in her tracks and takes in my ice-cream. "Enjoying yourself?"

The sun beats down on us. There's not a cloud in the sky, and I'm nursing a sense of well-being. I give her a wide, cheerful smile. "Well, I really prefer to be licking something else, but since you're not offering, Dakota..." I wink at her. "I have to make do with ice cream."

She goes red, and then she laughs and shakes her head. "Do you ever give up?"

"Admit it. If I did, you'll be bored."

She laughs again. "I would be bored," she agrees.

My ice cream is melting. Some of it drips down the side of the cone. Dakota scoops it up with her finger, and then puts it in her mouth and sucks, smiling wickedly at me.

I shake my head, my lips curling into a grin. "Bad girl."

"Very tasty," she purrs. "I'll see you around, King."

I think I'm in love with her. "I like that you're calling me King. Do that when we're in bed again, will you?"

Her eyes dance with amusement. "In your dreams, wiener-boy." She turns around, flips me off over her shoulder, and walks away.

I head back home, a smile on my face. It's going to be a good week.

12

DAKOTA

For the next two weeks, Julian King is everywhere.

When I'm not running into him, I'm hearing about him. I walk into the Daily Grind coffee shop one morning, and Sherri is there, talking to Kellie Krasinski. She waves me over. "Did you hear what Julian King did?" she asks, looking ready to burst with the news.

"Not a clue. Odd as it may seem, I don't keep track of Julian King's movements."

I think you're protesting too much, Dakota.

Kellie gives me a strange look, but thankfully, Sherri, who's by far the bigger gossip, doesn't notice. Instead, she fills me in on the situation. "It all started when Roger Wexler turned down Beth Shepperd's permit," she says. "I helped her file it myself; everything was done correctly. Roger was just being difficult."

No surprise there. Wexler is a petty douchebag. Still, even for him, this is too much. First the lowball offer, and now this.

"Poor Mrs. Shepperd," I say sympathetically. I can relate

to the Town Council's capricious whims. "I guess Roger took a dim view of her turning down his offer."

"Oh, he did more than that," Sherri says, her voice vibrating with anger. "It turns out that The Frozen Spoon had already been granted a permit to use the deck. Jim filed the expansion request when he got a permit to build the deck, two years ago."

I frown. "Then why...?"

"I checked the records myself," Sherri continues. "But the permit approval notice wasn't there. Somebody took that record out from our files. If Julian King hadn't found a copy, Mrs. Shepperd would've never known that her permit had already been approved."

My mouth falls open, as does Kellie's. Surely Wexler wouldn't... "Are you saying what I think you're saying?"

"I can't prove it," she says. "Nobody knows where the permit approval went."

"How does Julian King fit into this story?" Kellie asks.

"He's Beth Shepperd's lawyer. He wrote to the city, threatening to sue. The full Council met when they received his letter. They freaked out. Sally McKee looked up Julian's record as a litigator. Do you know, he's never lost a case?" Sherri shakes her head. "Sure, Wexler owns half the town. But still, what the hell is he doing messing with somebody like that?"

Wexler thought he was messing with somebody who couldn't fight back. He would have got away with it too, if Julian hadn't stepped in.

"Let's just say Roger Wexler won't be making any unilateral decisions anytime soon. The council wrote Beth Shepperd an apology, and also refunded her the fines they'd already collected for the state of her lawn."

Once again, Julian King is the town hero.

That weekend, The Frozen Spoon officially opens for the first time in the season. The deck is draped with bunting, loudspeakers play music, and it's a party. Mrs. Shepperd, looking happier than I've seen her in the last year, hands out samples of her sinfully delicious ice cream to everyone who drops by. Julian's there, leaning against the deck railing, smiling lazily, another ice-cream cone in his hand.

I walk over to him. "I wouldn't have pegged you as an ice cream type."

He smiles easily. "I like sugar."

"I heard you saved Mrs. Shepperd's store."

"Hardly. I wrote a letter. It took less than an hour."

"That's good. What do hotshot Toronto lawyers bill for that?"

He licks the ice cream, and my insides tighten. *Damn it, King. Why the hell are you so irresistible?* "I wouldn't know," he replies. "I'm retired." His eyes twinkle. "I make sausages now. Perhaps you've heard of my business? It's called the Sausage King." His lips twist up. "More meat than you can handle."

"You're not getting paid for your legal work?"

"I always get paid." He holds his cone out. "A lifetime supply of ice cream, that's what I was promised."

I have to laugh. "You're getting paid in ice cream?"

"Mm-hmm. Incidentally, if you're going to do that thing with the ice cream and your finger again, stand in front of me, will you?"

"Why?"

He fixes his chocolate brown eyes on me. "This is a family-friendly establishment, Dakota. There are children around. It's an inconvenient place for an erection."

I swallow hard at the heat in his eyes, the ragged edge in his voice. I want him. He seems to want me too. *Maybe we could date and see where this thing between us can go.*

There's a part of me that's always been reluctant to get involved with anyone. I don't need a therapist to realize that it's because of the way my father left. It wasn't just that he wasn't around. It was the cold-blooded nature of the act. He woke up one morning, decided he was done with his wife and family, and just walked away.

It's that same part of me that dismisses Julian's interest. He just wants what he can't get, I've decided. He likes the chase. The moment I give in, he'll lose interest.

But maybe I'm wrong.

"The first round is next week. Are you ready?"

"Absolutely," he says. "I went online and ordered an apron. It's short, frilly, and red." He lowers his voice. "You'll look sensational in it, Wilde."

I give him an exasperated look. "Don't get ahead of yourself. You still have to cook, you know. You're going up against people who have been doing this longer than a year."

He gives me a lazy smile. He licks his ice cream again, and my skin prickles with desire. Heat shivers through me. "I'm looking forward to it," he says softly.

Me too. I try to think of all the reasons I shouldn't be with Julian, but nothing occurs to me. I'm looking forward to the first round. I'm secretly hoping he won't be eliminated. I want to lose the bet. I want to end up in bed with Julian again.

The intensity of my need takes my breath away.

Dakota, I tell myself. *You're screwed.*

THE DAYS SPEED by in a blur of renovations, tourists, unreliable suppliers, and staffing problems. Teresa Barbini, who is my most reliable employee, twists her ankle, and I have to cover for her in the kitchen for three days until she is well enough to walk again. Nothing out of the ordinary.

Before I know it, it's the Friday of the first round of the contest.

The five of us show up at Haslem Park. When the council had sprung their Great British Bake-Off homage at us, I'd been too taken aback to pay attention to the other restaurateurs, but today, I take stock of them.

Marvin Hale, who represents The Friendly Crown, a chain of generic pubs scattered all over the province, is skinny, about five-ten, with greasy hair and ears that stick out. He's wearing a faded Metallica t-shirt and jeans.

At least he has good taste in music.

Valentina Greyson is about my height. Great boobs, fantastic ass. Her straight blonde hair is pulled back in a tight ponytail, and she looks focused and ready.

Don Mazzio of We Knead Pizza is a big guy. He's six feet tall. His shoulders are broad, and he looks like an aging linebacker, his muscles turning into fat. "This is stupid," he murmurs to me. "It's Victoria Day weekend. The tourists are out in force, and we're wasting our time here."

Tell me about it, buddy.

Rana's already at Haslem Park when I arrive, as are the filming crew. She introduces us to the judges. "There's going to be three of us," she says. "Chef Sarit Onruang, the head chef at *Nam Pla*. Mark Miller, a producer at Television Ontario. And finally, me. Of course, we won't be judging your food as much as enforcing the contest rules and making sure everything's going smoothly. Our opinions aren't the ones that matter. It's how well your food resonates with the crowd that counts."

The next step is to look over our ingredients and audit our receipts. Mark Miller looks at my stuff. "What are you making?" he asks. "Pizza, of course, I know that. What kind of toppings?"

"I figured I'd stick to the classics," I reply. "I'm making a sausage, prosciutto and mushroom pizza, a four-cheese blend with pesto, and finally, a margherita with tomato sauce, buffalo mozzarella, and fresh basil."

"Very nice," he says approvingly. "And for the sausage, are you using your competitor's product?"

Julian overhears us. "Dakota isn't interested in my wares," he says. "*Yet.* I'm hoping to change her mind this weekend."

He's not talking about his sausages. I return his glance, my throat dry. This time tomorrow, the first round will be over. And, if Julian doesn't get eliminated, I've agreed to go over to his house and cook dinner for him. *Naked.*

I'd tell myself it's irritation that's making me flush, but I'm not that good a liar, especially to myself. Anticipation claws through me, restless, eager, impatient.

Last year, almost to the day, I'd ended up in bed with Julian for the first time. A year later, and need still courses through my blood. I thought that time would temper my desire. It has not.

I force my attention back to the contest. Even though this evening is prep work, and we're not serving food, a crowd has gathered at the park. People have brought picnics, folding chairs, blankets, and frisbees. A group of teenagers is kicking around a football.

Dom and Cat are here too. "Come on, Dakota," Cat calls out. "Show them what you've got."

I laugh at her enthusiasm and wave to her. "Okay," Rana says, once the ingredient check is complete and the camera crew has set up their equipment. "Let's get going." One of the television people hand her a microphone. "Ladies and gentlemen," she says. "I'm delighted to announce the First Annual Madison Cook-Off. For three weeks, our contestants are going to dazzle us with their food and wow us with their creativity."

Umm, okay. Also, *First Annual Madison Cook-Off?* This is going to be a recurring event? Kill me.

"Tonight," Rana continues. "Our contestants will be prepping their food. Our two pizza makers will be working on their dough. Valentina is making tacos, and she'll be making her corn tortillas from scratch."

I suppress a snort. Valentina might be making fresh tortillas, but La Mesa, the chain restaurant she's representing, definitely does not. I've eaten there. The portions are huge, but the flavor is underwhelming. Yes, I know that makes me sound like a total snob, but trust me, my snark is justified. Everything I've eaten on their menu is bland and tasteless.

"Julian will be grinding meat and stuffing his sausages tonight," Rana continues with a straight face.

She's a better person than me. She says 'stuff his sausages', and I can't hold back my giggle. Julian hears me and grins. "You're becoming as bad as me, Wilde," he murmurs under his breath. "I love it."

I blush like a giddy schoolgirl. Gah.

"And finally, Marvin will be making burger patties. They have four hours tonight." She looks around at us. "If you're all ready?"

I nod, stomping on my wayward thoughts. *Focus, Dakota.*

"Let's get going. You may start... now."

13

DAKOTA

I t's a little tight with all five of us. As we get underway, it quickly becomes clear that Don has very little experience working in a kitchen. The guy looks completely frazzled. He keeps looking at his recipe, his face red and his forehead beaded with sweat. He almost forgets to proof his yeast. He puts his bags of food on the floor next to him, and more than once, he trips over them.

He looks terribly out of place.

Julian notices too. He catches my eye and winks. "Apron," he mouths.

Jerk.

I get to work, proofing my yeast, sifting flour and salt, adding water to make a dough. We're expecting four to five hundred people tomorrow, and I'm making enough food for a hundred and fifty of them. To help speed up the process and make the kneading easier, I've got my stand mixer fitted with a dough hook. I let it work, and when the dough looks ready, I turn it out onto an oiled bowl, cover it with a muslin cloth, and put it in the oven to let it to rise.

Then I look around again to see what everyone else is up to.

Julian—of course I'd look at Julian first—is feeding meat through a grinder. So many jokes there. No doubt, he's thought of all of them.

Marvin is shaping ground beef into patties. He's making sliders, so of all of us, he has the least amount of prep.

Valentina is making tortillas, alternating rolling out the dough and cooking them on a griddle, her movements smooth and unhurried. I can smell the delicious aroma of slow cooking pork coming from her station, and my mouth waters.

Don finally has his food processor running. I shake my head. He's way behind. He's going to run out of time.

Speaking of time, I better get a move on. I still have to make my tomato sauce.

Chef Onruang comes over to my station as I slice two dozen cloves of garlic, a camera guy trailing behind her. "You're using canned tomatoes?"

I nod. "This time of the year, fresh tomatoes just don't have the flavor they do later in the season," I reply. "At the peak of summer, we use local Ontario tomatoes, but the rest of the year, we find that canned tomatoes, especially the San Marzano, just taste better."

"I agree," she says. "Everyone tells me I'm being crazy, but to me, greenhouse tomatoes don't have the same taste as a sun-warmed, vine-ripened cluster." She steps away to interview Julian about his sausages, and I exhale a breath of relief.

DISASTER STRIKES as I season my sauce. I scoop a palmful of

red chili flakes into the saucepan, and, like a complete fool, touch my eye a few seconds later.

It feels like it's on fire.

Idiot.

I make my way to the sink, still clutching my jar of chili flakes. I rinse it out as best as I can, splashing water onto my face, cooling the reddened, burning skin. Eyes still watering, I head back, not paying very close attention to where I'm going.

Someone's barreling toward me. Don Mazzio, who's finally realized he's not going to be done in time. I dodge out of the way, and...

...collide into a broad, muscled chest.

Julian.

My jar of chili flakes flies out of my hands and slingshots into orbit.

Time slows down. I watch in horror as the jar start to fall. Chili flakes rain down.

Some of them land on the ground.

But most of the spice lands *in the bowl of sausage meat that Julian King holds in his hands.*

The crowd gasps audibly.

I clench my eyes shut and pray for the ground to open under my feet.

It doesn't.

"Really, Dakota?" Julian chides, his voice mild. "You're that afraid I'll win?"

My mouth falls open. I can't believe he'd think that I did that intentionally. My embarrassment drains away, and anger surges in its wake. "It was an accident," I snap. "I don't need to sabotage you; I'm perfectly capable of winning on my own."

"Whatever you say, Wilde." He goes back to the station,

and scoops the chili flakes out of his meat. I want to march over and give him a piece of my mind, but I'm conscious of the cameras recording, so I bite my tongue and look around for a dustpan.

Rana bustles over. "I'll handle the clean-up," she says helpfully. "You have less than an hour left. Get back to work, Dakota."

By the time we're done, my rage has drained away. I try to find Julian once I've cleaned up my station to apologize for the accident, but he's nowhere to be seen.

Maddening.

SATURDAY MORNING, we're back at it again.

I pull my dough out of the fridge; it's risen well overnight. I punch it down and set it to rise again. While it's doing that, I prep my toppings. I slice buffalo mozzarella, crumble feta and gorgonzola, and grate parmesan.

Julian looks like he made three different kinds of sausages yesterday. Right now, he's quick-pickling onions, cauliflower and carrots. His knife work is impeccable. I watch him slice the onions into razor thin rings, his eyes barely watering from the fumes, and nerves prickle my skin.

He looks just as home in the kitchen as any of us. Hell, he looks far more capable than Don, whose dough has barely risen overnight.

He told me that he knew what he was doing; I should have believed him. Julian King is not used to failing. He does everything with overwhelming competence.

Install a wheelchair ramp? No problem.

File a cease-and-desist against the city and get them to refund fines they've been charging Mrs. Shepperd? Piece of cake.

Give up your career, branch into something entirely new, and build a successful business in less than a year? Sounds about right.

It's infuriating.

You're obsessing about Julian King again, Dakota.

I turn my attention to the others. Valentina's chopping tomatoes, onions, and cilantro for a pico de gallo. Marvin is making coleslaw. Don is stirring his tomato sauce, a bored look on his face.

Ah. Tomato sauce. I get mine out of the refrigerator and set it on the stove to bring it up to room temperature. Almost from habit, I taste it before I spread it on my dough.

And I freeze.

Somebody has tampered with my sauce. It is sickeningly sweet. Vile. Somebody has dumped almost a cup of sugar into it, and it is inedible.

Salt, I could fix.

Sugar? I'm shit out of luck.

Cold realization spreads through me. Yesterday, Julian accused me of sabotaging him. Today, he's taken revenge.

Later, Dakota. For the moment, bury your anger and make a plan.

I signal to Rana. "I ran into trouble. Can I get somebody to run to the grocery store for some new ingredients?"

She considers my request, and then nods. "It'll still come out of your budget."

Phew. "I have room."

I gesture to Dominic, who's in the crowd. "Can you go to the store and get me a quart of cream, a couple of sticks of butter, a pound of potatoes and some rosemary?"

"What happened?"

I give my twin an exasperated glance. "Is now really the time for questions?"

"Fair enough," he says mildly. He disappears into the crowd. While Dominic is gone, I try to make a plan of action, but I'm shaking with anger and it's difficult to think.

This is Julian's doing, I just know it. He thought I sabotaged his meat yesterday, and to retaliate, he's dumped sugar in my sauce. I can't lose my shit right now; I have too much to do. But when I'm done here, I swear I am going to make him pay.

Ten minutes later, Dom's back with my supplies. "Thank you," I tell him fervently.

It's a mad scramble to the finish. I make a quick alfredo sauce, using the cream Dom just brought me and the parmesan I was planning to use in my four-cheese pizza.

The margherita will have to be scrapped completely, the tomato sauce is a critical ingredient. In its place, I'll be serving a potato and prosciutto pizza with alfredo sauce.

I assemble the four-cheese pizza—using the fresh mozzarella in place of the parmesan—while cooking the alfredo sauce.

I slice potatoes and sauté them with olive oil and rosemary. I make a hasty ragu-type meat sauce by chopping my last can of tomatoes and frying it along with the sausages and the mushrooms.

Have I done enough? I have no idea. For the next three hours, I can't think about anything. I just have to cook and serve my food, and hopefully, not get eliminated in the first round.

"Okay," Rana says cheerfully, her microphone in her hand, her voice carrying through the assembled crowds. "I know you're all dying to hear the results. But first, a round of applause to our contestants, who served us some amazing food today. The Sausage King, We Knead Pizza, La Mesa, The Friendly Crown, and Dakota's Pizza, thank you for your hard work."

Everyone claps.

Julian looks relaxed. I'm so angry, I can barely glance in his direction. "Now," Rana continues, beaming at the crowd. "The moment you've been waiting for. We've tallied up the ticket sales, worked out everyone's profit, and we've determined a winner. The winner of the first round is La Mesa. Valentina, congratulations. The tacos were a hit."

They did look amazing. La Mesa might not be a good restaurant, but there's no denying that Valentina Greyson can cook.

"Second place was a tie between Dakota's Pizza and the Sausage King. Dakota, Julian, congratulations. If it makes you feel better, it was really very close between the top three."

Had it not been for the last-minute expense of cream, butter, and potatoes, I might have won this round. I clench my hands into fists, and my blood starts to boil.

"Unfortunately, somebody has to come in fifth. I regret to say that the person who will not be joining us next week is We Knead Pizza. Don, I'm so sorry."

Don shrugs his shoulders. "What can I say? You win some, you lose some." He lifts his voice and addresses the gathered crowd. "Ladies and gentlemen, I am not the best cook there is, but I assure you, everyone in the We Knead Pizza kitchen, the real kitchen, is incredible." He holds up a stack of paper. "I have coupons here for a free small pizza at any of the five We Knead Pizza locations in the area. Please come and see me before you go, and I will give you one."

Huh. Smart. I feel a reluctant stab of admiration for Don, who is spinning his loss in the best possible way.

"Thank you, contestants. I'll see you in a couple of weeks for the next round."

It's over.

Rage still simmering in my blood, I clean up my station. Julian's gone by the time I look up. I go back home and take a shower to wash the smell of grease and garlic out of my hair.

Then, I get into my car and I drive to Julian's cottage.

The lights are off.

The asshole isn't at home.

I turn back to town. I'm determined to find him. I walk into the Madison Brewpub to ask Vicki if she's seen Julian anywhere, and who do I see the moment I walk in but the Sausage King himself, seated in a booth, a drink in front of him.

I walk up to Julian. "You sabotaged my tomato sauce," I snarl. "You deliberately put sugar in it so I'd be eliminated. This is how you want to play? Fine. From this point on, we're at war."

Julian looks up. I realize he's not alone. Sitting with him is Rana Halabi, and she has a drink in front of her too.

My red rage of anger evaporates.

He's on a date.

Bile rises at my throat. I feel sick to my stomach. Without another word, I spin on my heel and walk away.

Of course, Julian didn't wait for me, why would he? My own father couldn't be trusted to stay. Men don't stick around. That's been the lesson of my entire life.

14

JULIAN

Of course, I knew the chili flakes were an accident. When Dakota had run into me, she'd looked really horrified, and so I'd made a joke in an effort to lower the tension.

My humor missed its mark. She didn't think it was funny; she thought I was accusing her of sabotage.

When we were done Friday evening, I'd looked for her, but she was nowhere to be seen. Today, I tried to get a moment alone with her, but the damn camera crew was everywhere. Then, at the end of the contest, Rana had come up to me. "I'm meeting Luke for a drink at the Madison Brewpub," she'd said. "You want to join us?"

A cold beer had sounded really good. "One drink," I'd said. "I can't stay long." I had to go find Dakota and apologize.

She'd quirked an eyebrow but hadn't probed. We'd got to the pub and grabbed a couple of pints of Cat's excellent American pale ale while we waited for Rana's boyfriend to join us.

We'd been catching up when Dakota stormed in. You

sabotaged my tomato sauce," she'd accused, rage threaded through her voice.

Wait, what?

"You deliberately put sugar in it, so I'd be eliminated," she continues. "This is how you want to play? Fine. From this point on, this is war."

Then she turns around and walks out of the pub.

I'm so stunned I don't know how to react. I stare after her departing back. "Sabotage?" Rana asks. "What did she mean by that?"

"Not a clue. Someone put sugar in her tomato sauce, and she thinks it's me?" Does Dakota really think I'm capable of tampering with her sauce just so I win the restaurant permit? How ruthless and unscrupulous does she think I am?

You're taking advantage of Mrs. Shepperd's cash flow issues to force her to sell, my conscience uncooperatively points out. *That seems pretty ruthless to me.*

"She had to buy groceries today," Rana says thoughtfully. "She was planning to make a margherita, but she switched it up at the last minute. I was going to ask her about it, but she seemed stressed, and the producer thought Don Mazzio made for better television. The guy had no idea what he was doing."

"She thinks that I believe that she spilled the chili flakes on me on purpose."

Rana frowns. "Do you? She didn't. It was an accident. Mark, Sarit, and I discussed whether we should give you some extra time, but you seemed to handle it just fine."

"I know it was an accident. I scooped the chili flakes out, no biggie." I shake my head. When the fuck is Rana's boyfriend getting here? I need to go talk to Dakota. We spar verbally all the time, but this is different. "She thinks I was pissed enough about that that I would deliberately sabotage her? I didn't do anything to her damned sauce."

"Yeah, I know that. It's not your style. But somebody did." Her lips narrow to a thin line. "I don't like this. I'll review the tapes."

I look up. "You think one of the contestants did it?"

"I don't know," Rana replies. "Dakota's sauce was in the refrigerator overnight. The building was locked up, but the key is in town hall. Sherri keeps it in her desk drawer."

She's saying that a lot of people could have accessed the kitchen. But there's only one person working in the town council that's capable of active sabotage. "Wexler," I say flatly. "I know why he doesn't like me. But why would he go after Dakota?"

"You know what my dad would say," Rana replies. "Follow the money. We Knead Pizza, La Mesa, and The Friendly Crown all applied for restaurant permits. But where are they going to be located? There aren't many suitable buildings in town. We Knead Pizza is out of the race, but if La Mesa or The Friendly Crown want to open a restaurant here, they're going to have to rent space."

"And Roger Wexler owns half the town." I take a sip of my beer to calm myself. This is garbage. I don't care about my restaurant—I'm Type-A enough that I want to win the contest, but it isn't going to ruin me if I fail.

On the other hand, Dakota has a lot to lose. The gossip mills tell me that the building she's buying is in rough shape. Ben Watanabe doesn't come cheap. Then there's the property itself, right on Front Street. She would have paid a premium for it.

Dakota doesn't have parents who paid her way through law school. She doesn't have a grandmother who left her a cottage in her will. She doesn't have the cushion that eight years as an extremely well-paid lawyer have given me.

She's worked for everything she has. Now, the council is playing games with her life, and if that wasn't bad enough, Wexler's decided to play dirty.

I'm really, *really* tired of Roger Wexler.

Rana nods. "Exactly. You're planning on buying Mrs. Shepperd's property. Dakota bought Neil Silver's place. If either of you win, Wexler loses out on a lucrative tenant. He has everything to gain from seeing the two of you fail."

She's astonishingly well-informed. Then again, she works as Madison's social media manager. Being in the know is practically in the job description. "Enough to rig the contest?"

"Elections are in the fall," she replies. "Roger Wexler is not a popular councilor. He won't win reelection. He's got one chance."

I give her an amused glance. "You know, you would make an excellent lawyer."

She rolls her eyes. "Yes, I see how well that worked out for you. My dad still works eighty-hour weeks, and he's been a partner forever. No thanks, I'll pass."

"The contest..."

"I'll keep a much closer eye on it," she says, determination etched on her face. I'd tell her that she looks very much like Yossef, but she'd probably hit me. "We're attracting a lot of publicity with this contest. I've used my contacts to line up a production company that's willing to film it. If it gets out that the contest is being rigged, the fallout would be terrible."

A young man walks into the pub, looks around, catches sight of Rana, and heads toward us. "Is that Luke?"

She turns around, and her face splits in a smile. "Yes."

I get to my feet. "Good, I'll leave you with him. I've got to find Dakota."

"Of course, you do," Ronna says teasingly. "I noticed you couldn't take your eyes off her during the contest either."

"Will you cut it out?" I throw a twenty on the table, and head to the bar. Vicki's playing bartender tonight. There's an apron hanging on the hook behind her.

An apron.

She thinks you sabotaged her. She's not going to cook naked for you.

Yet, hope is all I have. I point to the garment. "Mind if I borrow this?" I ask Vicki.

She gives me a harried glance. It's Saturday night, it's busy, and they're short-staffed. She has no time to ask questions. "Not at all."

I grab it and make my way to Dakota's house. Taking a deep breath, I ring the doorbell.

She answers the door on the second ring. When she sees me, her expression turns stony. "What you want, Julian? You don't need to interrupt your date to give me some bullshit lie about how you didn't ruin my sauce."

My date? She thinks that was a date? *For the love of...*

I unclench my jaw. "Rana is the daughter of an old friend. She is not a date. If you walk by the Madison Brewpub right now, you'll see her having a drink with her age-appropriate boyfriend Luke."

Doubt flashes over her face. "She's very pretty."

"She is nine years younger than me. When I first met her, she was fourteen, and I was twenty-three. She wore pigtails, for fuck's sake. Dating her would be creepy." I stare into her eyes. "Once again, there's only one woman I'm interested in."

She bites her lower lip.

From the town gossip, I know her father walked out of her life when she was eleven. *Eleven,* I remind myself. I don't have the greatest relationship with my parents—they're a little too obsessed with the idea that their only child become a lawyer just like them—but though they weren't perfect, they provided me a steady childhood. They showed up to track meets. They didn't get up one morning and disappear.

Of course, she's gun-shy. I would be too, if I were in her shoes.

"I was a little homesick this evening. My friend Ward was supposed to visit this weekend, but his job got in the way." I don't like being vulnerable. I push through the fear. "Most of the time, I'm happy about my decision to leave Toronto and move to Madison, but every once a while, I miss my old life. When Rana invited me to join her and Luke for a drink, I went because she's part of the life I left behind."

"Oh."

There's another reason. This is Victoria Day weekend. This time last year, Dakota and I had hooked up. Three hundred and sixty-five days later, I still can't forget her. I can't get over her.

I don't want to.

"I didn't put sugar in your sauce. I know what happened with the chili flakes was an accident. I was trying to be funny; I failed."

"Okay."

Her expression gives nothing away. I should turn around and leave, but I stay. There's no room for misunderstandings here. Dakota is too important to me. "Does that mean you accept I didn't sabotage your sauce?"

She nods wordlessly.

"You trust that Rana and I weren't on a date?"

This time, her reply is so soft that I can barely hear her. "Okay."

I take another deep breath. She doesn't know it, but every time I flirt with her, I'm putting my heart on the line. She has no idea how much power she holds over me.

Man up, King. Nothing ventured, nothing gained.

"Excellent." I pull the apron out of my jacket pocket. "Because we had a wager, and I won." I hold her gaze. "If you want to get out of it, I'll give you one chance. You can tell me you're too chicken to carry through your end of the deal, and I'll leave."

I hold my breath and wait for her to reply.

She gives me a long look. Then she reaches for the apron. "Come on in, Julian."

15

DAKOTA

Who am I kidding? Of course, I'm going to invite him in.

For a year, I've been fantasizing about Julian. For a year, I've wanted another night with him. I'm tired of fighting how I feel. I'm tired of pretending I don't want this.

When I thought that Rana and Julian were on a date, I'd been upset and jealous. I'm not the jealous sort. When it comes to Julian King, my emotions are topsy-turvy. All my rationality goes flying out of the window.

Why is that?

There was no reason to believe that Rana and Julian are an item, and I'd still assumed the worst. There was no reason to think that Julian would have sabotaged my sauce, and yet, that's where my mind went.

I know why. I'm running scared. I throw up these barriers to drive a wedge between us.

It's too late. I'm already in too deep.

Tomorrow morning, I'll start over. Tomorrow morning, I'll push him away.

Tonight, I don't have the strength. He's at my door, holding an apron in his hands. He's told me something real about himself. It's a chink in the armor of Julian's overwhelming self-confidence, and it makes him human.

It makes him irresistible.

"I have some ground rules," I tell him. "This thing, whatever it is, it's just for tonight. It doesn't change anything between us. You and me, we're still in competition for that restaurant permit. I intend to beat the crap out of you. Tomorrow morning, we wake up, and go our separate ways."

Something flickers in his expression. "Okay."

He's standing in my living room. I don't know how to play this. Exactly a year ago, Julian King had been in my home, and I'd had the best sex of my life. More than that. Julian had been everything I wanted in a man.

A year later, that hasn't changed. I want him with painful intensity. My emotions are too close to the surface. My heart is exposed, and I'm terrified. It feels like I'm standing at the edge of an abyss, and I'm about to fall into a pit from which I cannot emerge.

I'm a minute away from turning into a blubbering mess. I'm fighting the urge to cling to Julian and beg him to never leave me, and I can't stand how vulnerable I feel.

He thought I was brave and fearless. I'm anything but that. If he only knew what a coward I really was, the look of admiration in his eyes will change to disgust. If he knew how fucked up I really am, he'd sneak out in the middle of the night. *Just like my father.*

Keep it light. Make a joke. This is Julian, remember? You can never go wrong with a sausage pun.

"So, Julian." I paste a bright smile on my face. "Are you going to stuff your sausage meat into my casing?"

He groans out loud. "That is a terrible line, sweetness."

"Admit it. You can dish it out, but you can't take it."

His lips twitch. "Take off your clothes, Dakota," he says with characteristic directness.

I take the navy-blue Madison Brewpub apron from him, my insides quaking with nerves. "I thought you said it was red and frilly."

"The one I bought online was, but it's also in my house. A fifteen-minute drive there, a fifteen-minute drive back." His eyes rest on me. "I was too impatient."

Warmth snakes through me. He wants me, and he's making no effort to pretend otherwise.

"Do you want a drink?"

"No more small talk, Wilde. I don't want a drink. I'm not hungry. Let's put our cards on the table. If you change into that apron, I'm going to spend the night, and I'm going to fuck you so hard that you will have trouble walking tomorrow. If you don't want that, if we're not on the same page about this, say the word, and I'll leave."

I have to give it to Julian; he doesn't play games. His straightforward honesty is... nice. Refreshing.

"You're saying that the whole 'cook naked for me and serve me wearing nothing but an apron' was just a pretext to get me into bed?"

He lifts his shoulders in a shrug. "Wasn't that obvious? Come on, Dakota. You aren't that naïve. We both know exactly what that bet was about. I want you, and you want me. Let's stop pretending."

"You're an arrogant asshole, King."

He grins. "You love that about me, Wilde."

As much as I hate to admit he's right, I do like this about Julian. I never have to pretend with him. I don't have to watch what I say. I don't have to hold back the snark; he can take it. I've always been myself around Julian King.

He's egotistical and conceited, but I never have to worry about protecting his fragile male ego. Julian is perfectly comfortable in his skin. He doesn't need me to clap adoringly and flutter my eyelashes at him to feel good about himself. His self-confidence is really, *really* attractive.

The night we slept together, I could tell him what turned me on. I told him how I liked to be touched, how hard I liked my nipples pinched. I told him he needed to pet my clit, coaxing it into the mood instead of going straight for it like a woodpecker tapping on a tree trunk. *Not that he needed that last bit of instruction.*

It had been the best sex of my life.

If Julian King is a drug, then I want another hit.

This is the moment of truth.

I lift my t-shirt over my head. I'm naked underneath.

Julian inhales sharply, his eyes hot with lust. Without taking his gaze off me, he shrugs off his jacket and throws it on my couch. He unbuttons his shirt, and his gorgeous, muscled chest comes into view.

"Your turn again," he says. "Lose the pants, Wilde."

"If you're going to order me around like this, you better deliver."

"I'll deliver." Not even a hint of doubt in his voice. He wags his fingers at me rebukingly. "Pants, Dakota."

Grr. Glaring at him, I push them down my hips.

His eyes turn hungry. "For a year," he murmurs. "I've been masturbating to the memory of you." He moves closer, and runs his hands over me, sliding past my waist to grasp my hips. His touch feels like fire. "The memory was amazing. The reality is so much better."

The way he's looking at me. The raw edge of need in his voice. I'm defenseless here. Need ignites in my blood. My knees shake. Anticipation grips me in its greedy claws.

"Now you." There's a quiver in my voice. My throat is dry. I'm soaking wet. My thighs clamp together. I'm so close to the edge, and he hasn't even touched me.

This makes no sense.

Nobody should have this much power over me.

He shrugs out of his jeans. His cock bulges obscenely. He's hard. Ready.

I don't want him. *I need him.*

"You unravel me, Dakota."

His words are simple. They echo through my mind and wrap around my heart. I tear them away. One night. Just one night.

His eyes glint wickedly. "Those are very sexy panties," he growls. "Black lace. Very hot. You can either take them off, or I can tear them off you. Your choice."

A full body shudder runs through me.

He gets naked. His cock is thick. Huge. Hung like a horse, I'd called it, and my memory hasn't exaggerated. My eyes go round. I can't tear my gaze away from him as I shimmy my panties down my hips.

"Like what you see?"

"Conceited jackass."

He laughs quietly. "Admit it, sweetheart. You're soaked for me, aren't you?"

"Not even a little," I lie.

"Liar." He yanks me into his body. My breasts grind into his muscled chest, and I shiver in arousal at the power in his grip. "You're telling me," he murmurs into my ear, "that if I pushed my finger into that tight little pussy of yours, I won't find you dripping?"

I double down. What can I say? I like to live dangerously. "That's exactly what I'm saying."

His lips tease the curve of my neck. His thumb strokes

my pulse. Then his mouth closes over mine, possessive, forceful, claiming. I gasp, and the last tatters of my resistance melt away. I kiss him back, moaning as need surges over me, my entire body prickling with desire. I wrap my arms around his neck and rub myself over his thick bulge.

I'm shameless.

I don't care.

His tongue slides into my mouth, demanding entry. I yield. My lips feel swollen and bruised, and oh-so-sensitive. His hand tightens in my hair, tugging ever so slightly. My scalp pricks with sharp needles of delicious pain. Forbidden heat floods through me, and I moan my arousal into his mouth.

I feel his kiss everywhere. Every nerve ending in my body comes alive. My toes curl, and my core tightens, and my body ignites.

He pulls back. His hot, hungry eyes bore into me. His nostrils flare. "I can smell your arousal, Dakota," he says. "You know what happens to bad girls who lie about how wet they are?"

He picks me up and carries me to my dining table. Wooden, heavy, and sturdy, it's the first piece of adult furniture I bought when I moved into this house. "I wanted to do this last year," he growls. He sets me down on the table. "Lie back, baby, and spread those legs for me. I can't wait to taste you."

A shiver wracks my body.

Oh God. He's going to eat me out.

He's going to eat me out on my dining table, and I'm powerless to resist.

His big hands lock on my knees. He spreads me open, and his hot, hungry gaze snaps to my pussy. "So fucking pretty," he murmurs. His fingers glide up my calves. Slowly, deliberately, he inches higher.

I writhe on the table, restless with need. Hurry up, Julian.

He spanks the insides of my thighs. "If you don't stay still, sweetness, I will tie you up."

Raw heat blazes from his eyes. His voice is saturated with dark promise, pouring gasoline on the flames of my arousal. I shiver again, ablaze with anticipation. "Julian," I whimper.

He gives me a smile of smug male satisfaction. "Yes, Dakota?"

Grr. I fall stubbornly silent, and he laughs at me.

I'm about to get off the table and march upstairs. I own a vibrator, damn it. I don't need to beg him for an orgasm.

Then his thumb presses against my aching clit. My back arches; I cry out. His touch sends me reeling.

Oh God.

Fuck the vibrator.

I'll never admit it to him, but this is so much better.

Julian's fingers shove deep into me. He strokes in and out of my pussy, his thumb pressing unerringly on my clit. Shivers wrack my body. I squirm on the table; I moan out loud. Intense need surges through me.

I feel the orgasm build at the edges.

I'm going to come so hard.

Then I feel his tongue swipes between my folds, and my arousal ratchets higher. Dangerously higher.

His mouth plunders me. His tongue dances over my aching, throbbing clit, exactly the way I like it. The speed is perfect. The pressure is magical.

Every muscle of my body clenches as I hurtle toward climax.

"Ask for it." His growl shocks me out of my haze of desire. "You want to come, you'll ask for permission."

I'm too far gone to flip him off. The need claws at me now, a wild animal tugging at its leash. Any second, it's going to break free and overwhelm me. Any second, this tsunami of pleasure is going to tug me under.

"Please..."

"Fuck, yes." His voice is ragged. He lifts his head, and I can see raw need in his eyes. He's making no effort to hide how much he wants me. "You have no idea how much I needed to hear that, sweetness." His gaze softens. "Come for me, Dakota."

I explode for him, shaking, writhing, moaning as I shatter over the edge. Fireworks explode. I drown in pleasure, gasping for more.

Julian's mouth stays on me. His talented fingers and mouth tease every quiver out of me, every moan, every shiver, until I can't stand it anymore. He changes position, looming over me, his fat cock nudging my lips.

"Open wide, baby."

Oh God, yes. I moan and lick my lips, wicked heat shuddering through my body. I want his cock down my throat. I want him to shove himself into my mouth and take his pleasure. I want to wreck him the way he wrecked me.

This angle, with him standing over me, I'm helpless to control how deep he plunges. Helpless to control how fast he thrusts. Thinking about it makes my insides twist and ache.

It's just one night, Dakota. Don't get used to this.

I swallow back the lump in my throat. "You want me to choke on your sausage?"

He groans. "Terrible," he says. "Wrap those pretty little lips around my cock, baby. Take me deep."

My tongue wets my lips. I open for him, and his fat head slide into my mouth. He throws his head back and groans, pleasure etched on his face.

That look on his face? It's because of me. Because of what I'm doing to him.

I take him deeper. His fingers find my nipples, and he tweaks them hard. I whimper around his thick erection. He remembers exactly how I like it. He's not being gentle; he's not holding back.

Tomorrow morning, when I put on my bra, I'll remember this moment.

When Julian King thrust down my throat and pinched my nipples hard enough to bruise them.

I keep my gaze on him. Opening my mouth wide, I take him as deep as I can, and his eyes blaze with heat. Over and over, he thrusts into my mouth, and I take him.

I feel naughty. Wicked. Powerful.

"Fuck," he snarls, pulling away. He's shaking. His control's hanging on by a very thin thread. "Oh no, Dakota. As wonderful as it sounds, I'm not coming down your throat. I've waited a year to sink into that hot, tight pussy, baby."

He grabs my hips and drags me off the table. "Bend over," he orders. "Spread your legs."

My tender nipples smash into the wooden surface. I feel his big, powerful hands grip my ass. I hear the tear of a condom wrapper. See the package flutter to the floor.

Then he slams into me in one deep, brutal stroke.

I cry out.

It feels right. It feels perfect.

It feels like coming home, and it terrifies me.

There's a large mirror in my dining room. I put it there to make the space look bigger. Now, I lift my head.

I watch him as he thrusts into me, his face contorted with pleasure.

I see myself, letting go and surrendering to him. I see the raw need in my eyes.

His thumb teases my puckered entrance. I stiffen, inhaling sharply.

"Is that a no?"

I consider his question. I've never done anal. I've always been curious, and I've always wanted to, but I've never trusted anyone enough to go there. Now, Julian's playing with my ass, and once I get past the shock of it, I'm both intrigued and turned on.

If there's one person I trust to make it good for me and to make sure I enjoy myself, it's Julian. For all his arrogance, he is an incredibly generous and considerate lover. He pays attention. He pushes me exactly as hard as I need to be pushed.

How far is he going to go with this?

How far will I let him?

"It's not a no."

He spanks my ass, hard. "Then relax your muscles and stop fighting it, Dakota."

"I've never done this. I don't have any lube."

"Don't worry." His voice is reassuring. "I'm not going to take your ass today." He flashes me a grin. "You set the pace, sweetness. If you want me to fuck your ass, show up at my door with a bottle of lube and ask nicely."

Oh, the incredible conceit of the man. "When pigs fly, King."

He just laughs.

He fills me, his cock in my pussy, his thumb in my ass. He takes me, he possesses me, he claims me. He wraps his free hand around my hair and tugs my head up. "Watch yourself," he growls. "I want you to see how beautiful you are. How uninhabited. How absolutely gorgeous. Look at how fearless you are. For a year, you've filled my memories, Dakota. For a year, I've thought of no one else but you. I want to see you fall apart, Dakota. I want to see your face when you come."

My breasts mash into the table. Each time he thrusts, my upper body is pushed forward, my nipples rubbing against the warm wooden surface of the table.

I don't recognize the creature I see in the mirror, a woman whose face is contorted with lust. A woman who moans in abandon, nothing held back.

He called me fearless, and for the first time, I see myself the way that Julian sees me.

"Touch yourself," he orders softly.

I move my fingers to my swollen clit. I stroke myself gently, shivers running through me. He's so deep. He pushes into me, and it's raw and powerful. My muscles grip him, quiver around him.

"I should make you wait," he murmurs. "I should take you to the edge, over and over. I should torture you the way you've been torturing me for the last year." He holds my gaze in the mirror. "But I'll be generous."

Grr. With superhuman composure, I refrain from strangling him. "I'll come whenever I want, King. Besides, my fingers are doing all the work."

"Really?" His eyebrow quirks. "My cock doesn't have anything to do with it?" He pulls out, and I almost cry. His thick head nudges my folds. "Go ahead," he invites, holding himself at my entrance with superhuman willpower. "Make yourself come."

"You don't think I can?"

"Of course, you can." His eyes meet mine. "I've touched

myself for a year, imagining this moment. For a year, I've fantasized about sinking into you. Feeling you quiver around me. I've fantasized about your soft moans. About the heat in your eyes. So you tell me. If you want to use your fingers, when there's a perfectly good cock waiting to make your fantasies come true, then knock yourself out."

The raw honesty takes my breath away.

"Asshole," I mumble.

He drags the head of his penis through my folds, and I break. "Please, push it in me. I want you."

"What was that, darling?"

If it wasn't for the moment of pure honesty that preceded this, I tell him to fuck off. He pushes in me, and I clench my muscles around him. He inhales sharply. "Fuck, that feels good," he groans. "I can't hold on, sweetness. I need you too much."

His thrusts turn wild and ragged. My fingers rub my swollen clit. His thumb fills my forbidden hole. It feels so wrong, but so weirdly arousing. Nerve endings I didn't know I had are tingling, and I feel so very naughty.

I give into the pleasure. My arousal builds. I stand on tiptoe and spread my legs wider. Over and over, he slams into me.

Then the dam breaks. I shatter. Pleasure floods through my body. My muscles quiver. My toes curl. Through my haze of lust, I hear him growl, and then he explodes.

I look at our reflection in the mirror. Great. Last year, we'd made love in the living room and in my bedroom. Now, I've added the dining room to the list. Every time I'm going to sit at this table, I'm going to remember this moment.

I'm going to think of him.

Julian King is imprinting onto my life.

My earlier bravery is gone. I'm just afraid.

"Give me ten minutes to recover," he says, running his fingers over my body, "And we'll do that again."

"Ten?"

"It's a little optimistic, I give you," he agrees. "What can I say? You make me optimistic, Dakota."

Goosebumps rise on my skin, and I shiver as his words penetrate my fog of lust. Nothing can come of this.

We're set up for conflict.

If I don't get that permit, I'm in serious trouble. I'll have to borrow money from my mom and from my brother. It'll take me a few months to sell Neil Silver's building, and I'll probably take a loss on it. I won't recover the money I'm paying Ben for the renovations.

If Julian wins the contest, would it change things between us?

I want to say no.

But I'm not sure.

I know that the people who deserve my anger are the five members of the town council, who are putting us through this ridiculous contest.

However, if Julian wins the contest, I know it'll impact the way I feel about him. It's bitterly unfair, but I'll blame him for my foiled expansion plans. Every time he talks about his restaurant, there'll always be a small part of me that will begrudge him his success, that will believe that it came at my expense.

This is your fear again, putting up barriers between you and Julian.

Maybe. Or maybe we're set up to implode.

Julian said he wants to date me. He's always direct; he's told me what he wants. The ball's in my court.

I'm not brave enough to take that next step.

Tonight is all I can have.

"Ten minutes? I'm going to time you."

He laughs, low and amused. "I'm insanely competitive, Dakota. I do my best work under pressure." He pulls me on top of him and presses a kiss to my lips. "I'll be ready."

16

JULIAN

When I wake up in the morning, her bed is empty.

It's deja vu all over again, but I'm not discouraged. Not after last night.

Dakota wants me. She might be afraid to take the next step, but she wants it.

I gave her a warning. I'm insanely competitive. I do my best work under pressure.

I intend to win.

Except I'm not fighting for the permit. I want something that's far more important.

I want her.

SOMEONE'S KNOCKING on my door when I get out of the shower. I wrap a towel around myself and head downstairs. It's Ward. "King," he says. "Do you know how long I've been knocking?"

It's *good* to see him. "You should have called."

"I did," he says pointedly. "I called last night to tell you I was going to be able to tear myself away from work; it went to voicemail. I've sent you five texts in the last three hours. Your phone is dead, Julian."

"Ah. Sorry. I hadn't noticed." I give him a sheepish look and step out of the doorway. "I was at Dakota's place."

He walks in. "I'm delighted for you," he says. "Now, put on some clothes, for fuck's sake. Then you can tell me all about it."

The sun is out again. It's promising to be a glorious day. I pull on a pair of shorts and a t-shirt, and head back down-stairs. Ward's looking out the window. "You've done a good job with the renovations. This place looks great."

"It feels good to work with my hands." I grab a couple of beers out of the refrigerator and hand Ward one.

He raises an eyebrow. "It's ten. Isn't it a little too early to start drinking?"

"It's a long weekend. We're on the beach."

"Those are valid arguments." He clinks his bottle against mine. "Tell me about the girl."

I fill him in. "I thought everything was going great, and once again, she left in the morning." I sigh. "Just like she did last year."

"Maybe she just wants sex," Ward says. "Maybe you're the one who wants more than that."

I shake my head. "That's not it. I've told her I want to date her. If she just wanted sex, she'd tell me. She doesn't do coy. It's one of my favorite things about Dakota."

"So instead she sleeps with you over and over and then runs away? She's jerking you around, Julian."

I glare at my best friend. "She's not jerking me around," I snap, immediately defensive. "Her dad left when she was eleven. Of course, she's going to have walls in place. Of course, she's going to be wary. I would too."

Ward gives me a smug grin, and I realize that the bastard was baiting me. "You're a jerk, Lewington."

"Takes one to know one. So, you're serious about her."

I nod. "I'm dead serious." I drain the beer. "But it's hard."

"Stop whining, King. It's not a good look." Ward softens his words by getting up to get me another beer. "Trust me, I know hard. Every time I see Dixie with Charles, I want to walk away. And yet, I don't."

"Why don't you?"

"Because it's worth it," he says simply. "I'd never made a move on Dixie while she's with Charles. That's not me. But if she breaks up with him..." His voice trails off.

"We're a fine pair, you and I."

He laughs shortly. "Since I don't want to talk about my problems, let's talk about yours. Life has been kind to you, Julian. No offense, but you've never had to really work for anything in your life."

My beer freezes halfway to my mouth. "What the hell?"

"Yes, yes, I know you put in a lot of hours at BCF. That's not what I'm talking about. Everything has come easy to you. Other people study for their LSATs, you saunter in and ace them."

I give my friend an irritated look. "That is a wild exaggeration."

He ignores me. "Other people have student loans; your parents paid your way through law school. Your mother and your father are both partners at two of Canada's most prominent law firms. Their connections opened doors for you."

"I didn't work at one of their firms," I say defensively. "I wanted to make my own way through life. That's why I went to BCF."

"You own your trial record. You're a fantastic litigator. Everything you achieved at BCF, you did on your own." He fixes me with an intent look. "But you didn't get that job on your own, Julian. Law's a small world. At that level, everyone knows everyone. You're Fredrick and Susan King's son. You could have screwed up that interview, and they would have still considered hiring you as an associate. They wouldn't have kept you around, but they would have given you a chance."

I want to refute what he's saying, but I can't. I'm painfully aware of my privilege. My mentor, Yossef Halabi, moved from Cairo to Toronto in the mid-eighties. He'd been the first non-white partner at BCF. He'd been handed nothing; he's fought for everything he's earned.

"Then your grandmother dies and leaves you this." He gestures to the cottage. "When you decide to leave law and start a business, you don't have to take loans like ordinary people. You have a nest egg to fall back on."

"I'm assuming there's a point to this apart from making me feel like shit?"

"Things come easy to you, Julian. And then there's this girl, and for the first time, it's not easy. So, you can either whine, or you can work for her."

"You're not listening to me. I'm ready to do whatever it takes."

"It might not work."

"It doesn't matter." It isn't going to be easy, but I can't think of anything I want more. I don't care if I'm having the same conversation with Ward five years from now. Dakota is worth it.

"No hesitation, King?"

"None at all." I lean back. "I need a plan."

You and me, we're still in competition for that restaurant permit.

I pull out my notebook. "The contest is putting us at odds," I say aloud, crossing out the Sausage King from my to-do list. "First step, I need to drop the permit application."

Ward looks up. "You're giving up the restaurant?"

"I told you, Ward. Whatever it takes." I frown in thought. A seed of an idea is taking shape in the back of my mind, but it's not there yet. "I'm not quitting the contest. Someone sabotaged Dakota yesterday. I want to be there to keep an eye on things. But yeah, the restaurant's off the list."

He gives me a disapproving look. "You made an offer to Mrs. Shepperd. If you back away from it, you'll put her in a bind."

"I'm not going to leave her hanging, Ward. I'm not backing away, not exactly. For starters, I'm not a total dick-head. Also, this town is Dakota's home. The people here are her friends. I'm not going to screw things up for her."

"What are you going to do?"

"Mrs. Shepperd doesn't really want to sell. She likes making ice cream and wants to let somebody else handle the business. She needs two things. Bridge financing, and a partner."

Ward quirks an eyebrow. "You?"

I shrug. "If she's interested, yes. There's nothing to it. She just needs someone to do her books."

He laughs. "I'm the accountant, not you. Taking over my territory?"

"God, no. You can keep your numbers. This is not complicated bookkeeping, Ward. I do it for the Sausage King. It's just keeping track of expenses, advertising ROI, that kind of thing. You could do it in your sleep."

"So that's the plan."

"It's the first part of it. I'm clearing the decks." I point my beer bottle at him. "I want Dakota. This is going to take all my focus. All my effort."

You and me, we're still in competition for that restaurant permit.

Not anymore.

Your move, Dakota Wilde.

17

DAKOTA

J ulian is gone by the time I get back.

He's received my message.

I know I should be relieved that he's not still here, but I feel empty inside. Drained. I feel like I'm stomping on something special.

I wish I wasn't such a pussy, but that's just the way it is. Things might be easier if I didn't love Julian so much...

I stop dead in my tracks.

Fuck.

Dakota, you fool. You've gone and fallen in love with Julian King.

I stagger to my couch and sink down on it. I stare blankly at the wall. I'm in love with him. After fighting it for a year, after avoiding him as much as I could, hoping the attraction would fade, I've still managed to fall for Julian King.

Of all the stupid things to do, this has to be the stupidest.

My phone rings. It's my mother. "Dakota," she says, sounding harried. "Can you grab some hamburger buns at the store on your way here? It's such a nice day, I thought we'd grill burgers and eat on the deck."

Crap. Lunch with my mother. A Sunday staple. I totally forgot all about it.

There's part of me that wants to call it off, lie in bed all day, and wallow in my misery, but if I bail, my mother will have a million questions. "Sure."

AT LUNCH, the main topic of conversation is the contest. "What really happened yesterday?" Dom asks me. "Why did I need to run to the store in the last minute?"

I explain about the sauce. My mom, Dom, and Cat look appropriately horrified. "I got to the park close to the end," my mom says. "I missed all that." She gives me a proud smile. "And despite that, you finished second?"

"Do you know who did it?" Dom says. "Was it King? Do I need to punch him in the face?"

I give my twin a death glare, but it's too late. My mother leans forward. "Julian, that nice young man who made sausages for Elise's party?" She frowns in puzzlement. "I thought the two of you were friends, Dakota. Why would he sabotage you?"

I swear I'm going to make Dom pay. As soon as I get done with this conversation, I'm bringing the topic around to grandchildren. Yes, that screws over Cat a little bit too, but she made her choice when she got engaged to my brother.

"No, Julian didn't sabotage me. That's not his style. It was probably one of the other contestants. I'll just have to be careful not to leave my stuff unattended." I shrug, hoping they'd drop it. "The Alfredo was a huge hit, and so all's well that ends well."

I'm about to bring the topic around to babies when Dom

glances at his phone. "Oh, would you believe it?" he says innocently. "We have to go. Cat needs to stop in at the brewery." He gets to his feet and kisses my mother. "See you next week."

Coward.

Not only is he running away before I could get him in trouble, but he's also leaving me with my mother, who has a look on her face that I know is trouble.

So far, Sandra Flanigan has been distracted by other things. She's in a new relationship with Tim Pollard. She's planning Dom and Cat's wedding, and she's got grandbaby fever.

I've been able to coast under the radar.

Now, thanks to my idiot brother, I'm front and center. Whether Dominic mentioned Julian inadvertently or not, I'm going to kill him.

"Sit with me for a bit, Dakota," my mother says.

Yeah, that's not a request. I pour myself a glass of water and brace for the inquisition.

It doesn't come. "When your father left," she says instead, her expression distant and oddly wistful. "I swore I wouldn't let something like that happen again. I swore I'd never allow myself to be hurt as badly as he'd hurt me. I excised love from my life. My focus was on the two of you."

She sighs. "It wasn't until much later that I realized that I was doing the two of you a disservice. I was a terrible role model to you and Dom. Because of me, both you and Dom have spent your adult lives avoiding commitment."

"Dom's getting married."

"Despite the odds, yes." She looks at me. "And then there's you, Dakota. You're like me. You love deeply, and because of that, you're afraid to love."

"I don't..."

She holds up her hand. I shut up. "I mourned your father for a year. Then I started getting angry. What kind of man would walk out on his wife and children without a word? Your father didn't deserve my love."

"You're right about that."

"And yet, for nineteen years after that that realization, I stayed single. Every time Tim asked me out, I said no. Even when I had my heart attack, and realized that life wasn't going to wait around, I didn't act. That was how afraid I was."

I glance at my mother. "What happened this year to change your mind?"

"Tim had a health scare. The doctors found a tumor. For three weeks, I thought I was going to lose him before I had a chance to tell him how I feel about him. I looked at the wasteland my life would be if Tim wasn't there, and I realized my fear didn't matter. We found out it was benign, and I knew I couldn't waste any more time."

"I didn't know."

"Tim wanted to keep it quiet. He told Elise, but that was it." She's quiet for a long minute. "I would never tell you to be with somebody that would cheat on you, or who would treat you with anything other than the utmost respect. But there are also no guarantees in life."

I nod wordlessly.

"You're an adult; you don't need your mother to tell you what to do," she continues. "I'm incredibly proud of everything you've achieved in your life, Dakota. You don't need to be married. You don't need a husband. You don't need a man to make you happy." She gives me an intent look. "But if you find somebody that's worthy of your love, Dakota, then you should take a chance. Because life is precious and fleeting, and I don't want you to look back twenty years later and wish you hadn't wasted your life being afraid."

I swallow hard. "It's scary."

"I know, honey." She pats my hand. "Trust me, I know. I've been there. But not everyone is your father."

I give her a sidelong look. "The entire town talked about us. We were the biggest topic of gossip in Madison."

"So what?" Sandra asks. "People talked because what your father did was so shocking. They were horrified. Anyway, surely I haven't brought up a daughter who cares about what other people think of her."

So far, I've made Julian do all the work. I've let him chase me. I've been capricious and coy, and honestly, I've been a pain in the ass. It's a miracle Julian hasn't told me to fuck off.

It's time for me to put myself out there.

I get into my car and drive to Julian's cottage.

There's a car in the driveway when I get there. He has a guest.

Familiar fear cloaks me. I ran away from him once again this morning. He must be sick of me by now. Has he found a replacement already?

No. With grim determination, I grind my fear into the ground. *Julian wouldn't do that. If he was done with me, he'd tell me. He wouldn't avoid the difficult conversation.*

I get out of the car, walk up to the front, and ring the doorbell. For a couple of minutes, nothing happens. My throat goes dry. I contemplate running away.

Then Julian opens the door. When he sees me, a smile breaks out on his face. "Hey, Dakota."

The tight knot of fear in my stomach melts away at that smile. "I should have called. You have a guest?"

"It's just my friend Ward. He was able to get away from

work." His eyes are warm. "It's really good to see you. Come on in."

He takes my hand and leads me inside. I look around the cottage. There's a main living room with high cathedral ceilings, a wrap-around screened in porch, and then a tiered deck that steps to the water. "Wow, this is really nice. Was all of this here?"

"No, I've been teaching myself to build stuff."

Of course he has. Typical Julian King. "Let me guess. You were bored."

"It was a very long winter," he grins. "I had to do something to keep myself occupied. I'd have preferred to warm your bed, but..."

"Idiot."

He laughs. "Beer?"

"I guess I can have one and still drive back."

"Or you could spend the night."

He's still holding my hand. His touch feels warm. Solid. Strong. "I'd like that."

He caresses my cheek. "Good." He leans forward and kisses me. "I'm fighting the urge to ignore Ward, drag you upstairs, and make love to you."

My breath catches. My nipples harden. "That's a very tempting image, but I want to meet your friend."

He opens the refrigerator and hands me a beer. "Come on then."

We head outside. Ward stands up with a smile. "You must be Dakota," he says, shaking my hand. "Ward Lewington."

The three of us fall into conversation. Ward Lewington has broad shoulders, blue eyes, and a very dry wit. "Tell me," I ask him. "Did Julian go around calling himself the King in Toronto?"

Ward laughs. "Only when he got very drunk."

I lean forward, fascinated. I don't think I've ever seen Julian even the slightest bit tipsy. "He got drunk?"

"It was a legal tradition," Julian says, putting his arm around my shoulders. "People bought you shots when you won a case." He smirks. "I won a lot."

"And there it is," Ward rolls his eyes. "The Julian King ego."

He's holding me, and it feels really nice. I rest my head on his shoulder, and for a second, I sense I've taken him by surprise. Then he smiles, and laces his fingers in mine, and life is good.

"So, Dakota. Julian tells me you're planning on expanding your restaurant?"

My good mood fades. "If I win the contest."

"You need a permit even though you already have one?"

"It's because it's a separate building," I explain.

"Could you build a walkway between them?"

I tilt my head to one side, considering it. "I could," I say thoughtfully. "But it won't do me much good. I'm licensed for forty seats, and I doubt they'll increase my capacity. No, I'll just have to win." I wink at Julian. "Sorry, King."

He grins lazily.

"Have your parents visited?" Ward asks Julian.

He stiffens. "No," he says shortly.

I give Julian a curious look. "They're not happy that I quit law," he explains. "They think it shows a lack of dedication and perseverance. Only losers quit."

"Your parents think you're a loser?" I give him an incredulous laugh. "How the hell did they reach that conclusion? Julian, you're good at everything."

Ward groans out loud. "Dakota, what are you doing? Don't feed his ego."

I wait for Julian to say something cocky, but he keeps quiet. "Would your parents come down if you make the finals?"

"I don't know," he replies, getting to his feet. "Want another beer?"

Huh. His parents are clearly a sensitive topic. I drop it. "Yes, please."

WHEN THE MOSQUITOES come out in force, we retreat inside. Ward yawns. "I'm wiped," he announces. "I'm going to bed. Dakota, it was a pleasure meeting you."

"Likewise." I really like Ward, but I'm dying to get Julian to myself.

Ward goes upstairs. I glance at Julian. "I have to work tomorrow," I tell him. "I'll be getting up really early."

"You need to leave now?"

I shake my head. "I'm going to disappear before you wake up. But this time, I'm warning you in advance."

He laughs quietly. "I appreciate it." He takes the beer from my hand and sets it down on the counter. "Come to bed, Wilde," he whispers in my ear.

My entire body ignites at the look of heat in his eyes. "Show me what you've got, King."

18

JULIAN

Last night, we were up until dawn. Over and over, we reached for each other. I had a year of suppressed lust to make up for. It was fast and furious, intense and wild and hot.

Last night, I'd wanted her with a burning desperation that had almost undone me.

Tonight, I can take my time.

Tonight, I intend to explore every inch of Dakota's body.

Make her moan for me.

Make her whimper.

I undress her slowly. She tugs my shirt over my head and I get rid of my shorts. Her gaze moves over my chest, down my abs, and linger on the bulge that's tenting my briefs, naked appreciation in her eyes.

Fuck me, that's hot.

"Like what you see?"

"Mmm. I'd like it even better if you took off the briefs." The tip of her tongue swipes over her lower lip, and I groan out loud. "I want to suck your cock."

She's going to be the death of me.

I pick her up and set her on the bed. "Wrap your fingers around the slats of the headboard, sweetness," I tell her firmly. "And don't let go."

"Or what?"

"Or I'll tie you up, and I'll tease you all night long, and I promise you, you won't come until sunrise."

Her eyes flare with heat. She swallows hard and moves her hands over her head, her fingers gripping the headboard. "That sounds... tempting."

God, she's perfect. Wet and open for me, naked, beautiful, gloriously uninhabited.

I kiss her, deep and long, our tongues tangling, my hand cupping her breast. I graze her nipple, and she whimpers. "They're sore today. Go easy on them."

I prop myself up on an elbow. "Was I too rough yesterday?"

"Hell, no. It was great. It was exactly what I need."

I suck the swollen nub gently into my mouth. She throws her head back, her hair spreading in glorious waves all over the pillow. "Ah, that's perfect."

The raw edge of need in her voice... My cock hardens. I push her breasts together and bend my head over the delectably perky tips, dragging my tongue from one to the other.

She inhales sharply. "Do that again."

Anything for you, Dakota.

I kiss her neck, her throat, her nipples. I tongue her belly button and she arches toward me, giggling a little. "That's ticklish."

I do it again, and she laughs breathlessly, and the sound sends a hot wave of arousal through me. I make my way down her body and spread her legs. She's wet, so wet. I taste her, my tongue slowly dragging through her pretty pussy, and she groans again. "King," she whimpers. "What are you doing to me?"

Making her come.

I lap at her clit and pump my fingers in and out of her slick, wet heat. She grips the slats, her back arching with pleasure. "Julian," she breathes, and the sound of her voice moaning my name is sweet music to my ears.

She's here. In my bed. Crying out my name. It's almost unbelievable. It's the hottest thing in the world. It's better than any fantasy I've ever had.

"I'm coming," she wails. I suck her swollen clit between my lips and she flails, and she explodes.

Fuck me, that was hot.

I roll a condom on and slide into her. She's hot and tight and so fucking wet that I almost come right there. I grit my teeth and think the most unsexy thoughts I can, and wait for the urge to explode to pass.

Then I start to thrust. "Yes," she moans. "Harder."

I pull back and slam back in. "That hard, sweetness?"

"Yes," she whimpers, her eyes wild and her breathing ragged. "Just like that."

I push her legs in the air and stroke into her, over and over. Pleasure envelops me. Every time I hear her moan, I have to claw back from the edge. Every time she clenches her muscles, I grit my teeth in a desperate struggle not to come.

Not yet.

I grip her hips. She gasps, trembles. Her pussy milks my cock. "Fuck," I swear through clenched teeth. I stroke harder, her muscles quivering around me. Blood pounds in my ears. My fingers dance over her clit. My thrusts aren't controlled anymore. I see spots in front of me as I move faster and faster.

My world narrows to her, to the feel of her body under me, to the sounds of her moans. Then my body stiffens and, just as her climax overtakes her, I erupt.

Against all odds, Dakota is in my bed.

I want more. I want her in my life.

Now, I have to do what it takes to make that happen.

19

DAKOTA

Dakota's Pizza is normally closed on Mondays, but because this is a long weekend, the rules have gone out of the window.

My alarm goes off at five in the morning. I crawl out of bed, trying to be as quiet as possible so I don't wake Julian, get dressed, and head downstairs.

The sun hasn't yet risen. It's still dark outside. I put on my jacket, and then I hear footsteps on the stairs.

It's Julian. "Hey," he says, his eyes still hazy with sleep. "You want a cup of coffee before you head out?"

Coffee sounds amazing. "Go back to bed," I urge.

Ignoring me, he starts grinding coffee beans. "Ward's a morning person too," he says, sounding resigned. "He'll be up soon enough."

"I'm not really a morning person," I tell him. "Left to myself, I'd lie in bed until ten."

He flashes me with a grin. "A girl after my own heart."

Once the coffee's made, we take our mugs out to the screen-in porch,, sit in rocking chairs, and watch the sun rise over the lake. The water is so calm that the surface looks like a mirror. The only noise is the chirping of birds. It's astonishingly peaceful. "I love it here," Julian says, echoing my thoughts.

"Is that why you quit your job? Because you got tired of the city?"

"Not exactly. Madison was a happy accident. My grandmother left me the cottage in her will." He sips his coffee. "Life was passing me by, and I was too busy to realize what I was missing out on. Too busy to even stop to think about what I wanted. I was on the treadmill, and there was no getting off."

He's in a talkative mood, and I'm going to take advantage. "What changed?"

"A few years ago, my father was diagnosed with testicular cancer. The day he was going in for surgery coincided with the opening date of a big trial for which I was one of the attorneys. It was made pretty clear to me that if I blew off the trial, I'd never make partner."

I give him a shocked look. "They can't do that, can they?"

"Officially, no. Informally? Everyone who competes for a partnership is exceedingly well-qualified. Who is to know the real reason they pick one candidate over the other? Anyway. That was the first sign that it wasn't the right path for me." His smile is wry. "I thought my parents would encourage me to quit my job, but they both insisted I attend the trial." He shakes his head. "Priorities."

When my mother got sick, Dom had moved back from Toronto. The two of us had adjusted our schedules so that one of us was always with her until she got back on her feet. I can't imagine how helpless I'd have felt if I hadn't been able to do that for her.

"The real kicker was that when my father got well again,

he went right back to working eighty hours a week. That was all he knew."

The sky is pink, purple, and gold. The sunrise is glorious. Sitting here, next to Julian, I'm glad I get to share this moment with him. It's weird that we're not sniping at each other. Weird, but also really nice.

"When I was in college," he continues. "I used to have hobbies and interests. Then I started working, and one by one, everything except work fell away. I could see my future, and it looked exactly like my father's life. I wanted something else. If I'd made partner, I would have never found the courage to leave. I walked away before I got to that crossroad." He grimaces. "As you probably realized from last night's conversation, it wasn't a popular decision."

He gives me a sidelong look. "What about you? What made you go into business for yourself? That couldn't have been easy."

"No, it wasn't, not at the start. There's no deep reason. The only jobs around here are seasonal. If I wanted to stay in Madison, I knew I'd have to go into business for myself, and so I did." I smile faintly. "I'm probably too opinionated and stubborn to work for somebody else anyway."

"Really?" His eyes dance with amusement. "I hadn't noticed."

"Jackass."

He laughs out loud. "I know that it's going to kill you to admit this, Dakota, but we're pretty identical, you and me. We're both competitive. Neither of us likes to lose. I'm not the only Type-A personality here."

I give him an indignant look. He just grins. "Fine," I concede. "I might be a little Type-A." I drain the rest of my coffee. "And on that note, I better get going. Pizza isn't going to make itself." I hesitate, and then plunge ahead. "You want to do something later this week?"

"Absolutely," he says. "I'm swamped on Tuesday. I've got deliveries to make, and once I'm done with that, I need to spend a few hours in the kitchen. How about later on this week?"

I check my schedule. "Teresa has a day off on Wednesday, so I'll be working. But I'm done at two on Thursday, if you're free."

"I'm free." He smiles at me. "It's a date."

A date. My heart squeezes. We'll go on a date Thursday, and then the day after, we'll be competing against each other for a restaurant permit. *And if I lose...*

I jump to my feet. I can't allow myself to freeze in fear. I won't let the town council and this stupid, ridiculous situation come between Julian and me. I'll have to do something.

I just don't know what yet.

THE RESTAURANT IS CLOSED; the kitchen is deserted. I turn the lights on, brew a pot of coffee, and get to work. I don't particularly like mornings, but there's something almost soothing about this time of day. The world is very quiet, very still, and very peaceful.

Or it would be, if it wasn't for this contest.

I proof the yeast and start the process of making pizza dough. As I work, I think. So much has happened in the last two days that I've barely had a chance to reflect on who might have sabotaged me and when it could have occurred.

It could have been Friday evening. Toward the end, when our allotted prep time was almost up, all five of us were hurrying back and forth between the ovens and the refrigerators. Don Mazzio was rushing around, not looking where he was going, completely flustered by the fact that he'd run out of time. More than once, Valentina, Marvin, Julian, and I had been forced to swerve to avoid colliding into him.

Then there had been the added distraction of the judges walking around and interviewing us. The camera crew, trailing behind them, wires everywhere.

It had been pandemonium.

It would have been the simplest thing to slide the lid of my saucepan aside, spill a cupful of sugar into my sauce, and walk away. It could have been done in ten seconds. Any one of the people there could have done it.

Then there's Rana's theory. Julian had told me about her suspicions yesterday, about how she thought that the crime had been committed once everyone had left for the night.

There's no way I can narrow it down. No way I can identify the culprit. I just have to put it out of my thoughts. The next round is in four days. This time, I'll just have to be more careful.

I chop garlic and crush tomatoes, all the while trying to think of a solution to my problem.

Could I give up my expansion plans?

My offer has been accepted, and I've put down a fifty-thousand-dollar deposit, drawn from my line of credit. I have no idea how I'll pay back the loan if I back away from the deal. Dakota's Pizza is profitable, but once I pay out salaries, suppliers, property taxes, and other expenses, it doesn't leave me with a ton of spare money. I certainly don't make enough money that I can take this kind of loss without batting an eyelid.

But I hadn't been the only person who had wanted to buy Neil Silver's building. Roger Wexler had been interested, as had a large coffee chain based in Toronto. The coffee chain had dropped out when they'd realized how much work it would take to get the place operational. Wexler had bailed when he discovered he had competition and wasn't about to snap up the place on the cheap.

Ben Watanabe has already completed some essential repairs. He's re-shingled the roof, and he's replaced the rotting wood planks on the wraparound deck. Perhaps he's done enough that the coffee shop chain would once again be interested in buying it.

If I sell, I'd not only take a considerable loss on the sale. I'd also kiss the dreams of expanding Dakota's Pizza goodbye.

But I won't be in direct competition with Julian.

He hadn't come out and said it, but winning the contest matters to Julian. His parents are a sore spot. On some level, his relentless drive to win must come from needing to win their approval.

All my adult life, I've put my business ahead of a relationship. This time around, I want to prioritize Julian King.

ONE OF THE line cooks calls in sick, and so I don't get back home until six in the evening. I take a long shower, and then, before I can talk myself out of it, I place a call to Neil Silver.

I get his voicemail.

"Hi, Mr. Silver," I say into the phone. I'm nervous about making this call. Neil Silver is both high-strung and litigious, and if I had any other option, I wouldn't call him. "This is Dakota Wilde. I'm not sure if you've heard, but the city of Madison has complicated the process of getting a restaurant permit. I was wondering if the two of us could talk about options."

There. That's nice and vague.

I leave my phone number, ask him to call me back, and then hang up.

I know I'm being crazy and impulsive. For a year, I avoided Julian, absolutely convinced that I couldn't keep him. That he'd walk away the moment I fell in love with him. That he'd leave, the way my father had.

But he's here. We're together. It's only been two days, but already, it's way better than I thought it could be.

I never thought I could have Julian King. Now that I do, I will do anything to keep him.

20

JULIAN

Tuesday morning, I get up, call Mrs. Shepperd to warn her that I'm coming over, and head to The Frozen Spoon. She's in the kitchen, making a custard base for her ice cream.

Her expression turns wary when I enter. "Julian. Is there a problem?"

I don't know. I think I'm making Beth Shepperd a fair offer. If I've read her correctly, she doesn't want to sell, and simply wants somebody to manage the business end so she can keep making ice cream. But I could be entirely wrong.

I've made contingency plans. If she wants to sell the place, then I'm still going to buy it. Elections are in the fall. This time next year, there will be a new set of councilors, and I'll revisit the idea of a restaurant permit. One way or the other, I'm going to make sure that Dakota wins this contest.

"I have a proposition for you."

She turns off the stove and takes the pot off the heat. "You do?" she asks, giving me her complete attention.

"Do you want to sell this place, Mrs. Shepperd?" I ask

bluntly. "If you do, I've made you an offer, and I will honor it. But if you don't, I have a proposition for you."

"A proposition?" Her shoulders are stiff. Her body, tense.

"Would you be interested in a partnership, Mrs. Shepperd?" Before she can answer, I plow ahead. "I'll be a silent partner. I'll front the money needed to fix this place up. I'll do the books and the paperwork, and handle everything on the business end. At any point of time, you can buy me out." I drafted a contract last night. I hold it out to her. "In exchange, I would take twenty percent of the profits."

She looks at me. "I don't understand. This place isn't going to make you rich, Julian. What do you really want?"

Dakota.

"Maybe I'm just safeguarding my lifetime supply of ice-cream."

She snorts. "I'm not a fool, young man. What's the catch?"

"There isn't any. I might not get the restaurant permit. I have no interest in making ice cream. I need to hedge my options. Plan A fell through; this is Plan B."

That sounds reasonable, right? Contingency plans, backup options, assorted business-speak. Nothing about Dakota. Nothing about the woman for whom I'll happily upend my life.

"You want to go into partnership with me."

"I've taken the liberty of drawing up a contract. Once again, there's no hurry. Take all the time you need to look it over."

She takes the contract from me and sets it down on the counter. "You already know that this isn't my strong point, Julian." She stares at me for a long minute. "Fifteen percent."

"Done." I pull a pen out of my back pocket, scratch out

the twenty percent figure on the contract, and write fifteen instead.

She stares at me. "I really don't understand you."

"I like to think of myself as a man of mystery," I tell her cheerfully. "Now, I'm your lawyer, but I can't look at this contract for you. It's a huge conflict of interest." I scribble a phone number on a piece of paper. "This is the helpline for the Law Society. They'll be able to direct you to a reasonably priced lawyer who can look over this contract. Don't pay more than five hundred bucks. Make sure that you understand what's involved, and make sure you're comfortable with the terms. If you need to change something up, I'm open to negotiation."

Hell, I'll do it for free.

She's not listening to me; she's still trying to figure me out. "Now, this wouldn't have anything to do with a certain young woman I saw you talk to on the deck the day I opened, would it?"

Dakota is private. Until she makes our relationship public, I'm not going to. I put on my best poker face. "I can neither confirm nor deny that."

She chuckles. "I'm not going to call the Law Society. You've been more than fair to me through this process. Let's shake on it, Julian."

"Sorry, no. As your lawyer, I'm going to respectfully suggest that you get this checked out. Please do your due diligence, Mrs. Shepperd." I hold out the contract to her. "And then, we can go into business together."

21

DAKOTA

Neil Silver doesn't call me back Monday. Not surprising; it is a long weekend after all.

He doesn't call me back Tuesday morning either. I spend the first half of the day getting caught up on paperwork, and head over to the Madison Brewpub at lunch to see Vicki and Cat want to take a break.

The two of them are sitting up front, a platter of sausages and cheese in front of them. "Dakota," Cat says with a bright smile. "Join us. We're tasting some additions to the menu."

"You already have a cheese plate, don't you?"

"The sausage is new," Vicki replies. "Julian made it using some of Cat's stout. He dropped off a batch last night, but neither of us have had a chance to try it. Sit down. Have some."

If Julian were here, he'd tell me to eat his meat, and I'd call him an arrogant dickhead. And then he'd kiss me, and I'd kiss him back...

"Dakota?"

I drag my attention back to my friends. "Sorry, what were you saying?"

Vicki gives me an amused smile. "Do you want some of this sausage?"

So many jokes. "Yes, please." I reach for a piece. *I should send him a photo of me stabbing his sausage with a sharp toothpick,* I think. *He'd find that funny.*

Vicki's saying something again. God, I'm a terrible friend. I yank myself from my daydream and focus on my friends.

"Oh my God." Cat's eyes go wide. "This is so good. Holy crap. I love Julian's sausage."

Don't laugh, Dakota. Whatever you do, do not snicker.

"Wow." Cat eats another piece with obvious relish. "This is so flavorful and juicy. Really moist."

Vicki looks like she's trying not to burst out laughing. I stare at Cat. Does she hear her words? Flavorful? Juicy? *Moist?* I can't decide if she's being serious, or if she's pulling my leg. Surely, she's not that naïve.

"It's got a really nice kick to it too," Cat continues enthusiastically. "Very spicy. Dakota, when you see Julian next, you have to tell him how good his meat is."

I almost choke on Julian's sausage. Ha ha. "What do you mean, when I see him next?"

She gives me a puzzled look. "You'll see him Friday night at the contest, won't you?"

I'm trying not to think about the contest. "You want me to walk up to Julian King, and tell him that you find his sausage juicy, flavorful, and moist." She's definitely pulling my leg.

Cat nods eagerly. "You forgot spicy."

Vicki explodes with laughter. Okay, okay," she chokes out. "I can't do this anymore. You're a freaking genius, Cat. You should have seen the look on your face, Dakota. It was priceless."

My cheeks heat. "You did this deliberately? Very funny, ladies. Hilarious."

Cat laughs. "I thought so." Her phone rings, and she gets up to answer it.

Vicki's still cracking up. "That was so awesome," she says. "Cat's poker face is amazing. I couldn't have done it."

"Everyone's a comedian."

She grins. "These are really good. I think we'll put them up as a special this week. A gourmet version of bangers and mash. Stout sausage, chive and garlic mashed potatoes, and maybe some farmer's market asparagus."

That does sound delicious. My mouth waters. I steal another chunk of sausage from the platter in front of me. I'm glad Vicki's laughing. She's been quieter than usual in the last couple of weeks, a result of her break-up with Liam. "How are you doing?"

"About Liam, you mean? I'm fine, I guess. It'll get better. Liam was a very nice guy, and I liked him a lot. But he wasn't the one."

I lift my head up. "The one? Is there such a thing?"

Yes, there is, my heart whispers. *Julian.*

"In general? I don't know. Specifically for me, yes. There's a guy. He's not available. He's never been available. But in the back of the back of my head, no matter who I'm in a relationship with, a part of me is always waiting for Will."

I stare at her. "Will, Cat's evil ex-boyfriend?"

She makes a gagging sound. "Do I look like I have terrible taste in men? Never mind, don't answer that. No, different Will."

I want to be nosy, but before I can probe further, there's a knock on the door, and Randy, the postman, comes in. "Here you go, Vicki," he says, handing her a stack of mail.

"Dakota, do you want me to drop yours off at your mailbox, or will you take them now?"

I reach out. "I'll take them."

He hands me three envelopes. I flip through it. Bill, bill, and an official looking envelope from the law offices of Duffy and Kane.

Why does that sound familiar?

With a sense of foreboding, I open the letter, and scan the contents. The blood freezes in my veins.

It's from Neil Silver's lawyers.

"Ms. Wilde," they write. "In light of recent events, Mr. Neil Silver has reason to believe that you will not be able to honor your commitment to purchase his Front Street property. As a result, Mr. Silver must regret to inform you that until the closing, you and your contractors will not be permitted access to the property. Furthermore, in recognition of the increased risk of you reneging on your agreement, we request an additional deposit of five percent. This money will be used to roll back the changes your contractor has made to the property if you fail to go through with the purchase. Please provide this payment immediately."

Fuck. Silver can't be serious, can he?

"Dakota, what's wrong?"

I hand Vicki the letter. She scans it quickly. "This is garbage," she says flatly. "They can't do this."

I brought this on. I was trying to prioritize my relationship with Julian, and this letter is a direct consequence of that. "I don't know." My voice is hollow. "It all sounds pretty official to me." My shoulders slump. "I guess I should talk to someone to find out if this is legal."

"Talk to Julian."

I look up. "Julian?"

She nods. "Yes, Julian King. I know you can't stand him,

but he is an extremely competent lawyer. Look at what he did for Mrs. Shepperd. Put aside your pride and ask him for help."

"I don't hate Julian," I whisper. "We hooked up over the weekend. I think we're dating now."

Vicki's mouth falls open. "That's fantastic news, Dakota. So, there you go. Ask him for help."

I wince. "I don't know, Vicki. We just started dating, and I already want him to solve my problems."

Vicki groans. "Do you like Julian?" she demands.

"Yes."

"Would he help?"

"Of course." He hides it under the most outrageous puns and more than his fair share of arrogance, but Julian's a good guy.

"Okay, then. Can I give you some unsolicited advice? Stop being ridiculous. You're in a bind. Let Julian bail you out."

22

JULIAN

After talking to Mrs. Shepperd, I head back to the cottage. Bypassing the house, I make my way to the commercial kitchen.

The long weekend messed up everyone's schedules, mine included. I normally do deliveries on Mondays. I'm a day behind, and I'll lose another half a day on Friday. I'm going to be scrambling like crazy this week.

I'm still the luckiest guy in the world.

With a smile on my face, I check my messages for any last-minute changes, and then load my truck. On a whim, I pack a cooler with a couple of lamb and harissa sausages, fresh buns, cheese, pickles, sauerkraut, relish, and mustard, as well as a couple of bottles of water. If I time my route right, I'll end up at the Madison Brewpub shortly before noon.

Maybe Dakota will be able to break for a picnic lunch.

Lady Luck is beaming down on me today. When I pull up at the brewpub, Dakota's there, talking to Vicki. "Hello, ladies," I greet them. "Vicki, you want me to put your order in the refrigerator?"

"That'd be great."

I turn to Dakota. "Will you give me a hand, Wilde?"

She laughs. "Is that your way of getting me alone?" She gets to her feet and puts her arms around me. Standing on tiptoe, she presses a kiss to my lips. "Hey, you."

I return her kiss. "I see you've told Vicki about us. I approve."

"Would you believe, whenever I'm planning to do something, that's the question that's on my mind?" she snarks. "Would Julian King approve, I wonder."

"Brat." I kiss her again, nipping her lower lip.

Vicki clears her throat. "Enough with the PDA, you two. This is a family-friendly establishment."

Dakota rolls her eyes. "Please. I've seen Dominic and Cat do this and more."

"Cat is a part-owner, and I can hardly ask her to tone it down," Vicki points out with a grin. "You two, on the other hand..."

I laugh and disentangle myself from Dakota. It takes a surprising amount of willpower. She's soft and warm, and she smells like roses and sandalwood, and I want to hold her. One of these mornings, the two of us are going to wake up at the same time, eat breakfast in bed, and then make love again. Maybe we can even get away for a couple of days. Not the weekend, of course; we both run food businesses in a tourist town. Going away for the weekend is a luxury that needs to be saved for the off-season, but maybe we can get away mid-week.

Once I'm done unloading Vicki's order, I turn back to Dakota. "Have you eaten?" I ask her. "I have food in the truck. Want to drive to Haslem Lake and eat lunch by the water?"

She nods. "Yeah, I'd like that."

"Excellent."

We drive down a deserted dirt road that ends in the water. I find a tattered blanket in the back of the truck, and I spread it on the sand. "Ta-dah."

Dakota grins. "My prince."

"King," I correct her. "Let's get this right, Wilde. I am the king."

She rolls her eyes. "What do you have for me, King?"

I wink at her. "A thick, juicy, sausage."

Her lips twitch. "Of course, you do. I demand foreplay first."

I open my cooler. "Lamb and harissa sausage, fresh rolls, and an assortment of fixings. Dig in."

"Nice." She shoots me a wickedly amused look from beneath her eyelashes. "Cat couldn't stop complimenting your sausage, Julian. She thought it was juicy, flavorful, and spicy."

My mouth falls open. "She said what?"

"Oh, she loves your meat," Dakota says innocently. "After she had your sausage, she said she felt really stuffed."

My food goes down the wrong way. I start to cough. My eyes watering, I reach for a bottle of water. "Cat said that?" Fuck me, I think I'm blushing. Also, Dakota's brother is going to kick my ass. "I don't know what to say. Listen, you know I only do the sausage puns with you, right? I don't go around telling random women to eat my meat."

She bursts out laughing. "You should see your face," she giggles. "Vicki and Cat pulled the same prank on me. They were sampling the stout sausage you'd made. Cat sat there, her face dead serious, and she told me she loved your meat, and she wanted me to pass the message on. For a few minutes, I couldn't figure out if she was joking or if she was serious."

I chuckle. "Funny."

"They certainly thought so." She falls silent, and then takes a deep breath and pulls a folded envelope from her jacket pocket. "Julian, I got this in the mail today."

I pull out the letter and read it, and my temper flares sharply. Neil Silver is taking advantage of the situation. People like him drive me nuts.

"I'm not hinting for help," she says. "I know you're retired. If there's a lawyer you can recommend…"

I look at her. "I'm a pretty good lawyer," I tell her. "I'd love to sort this out for you. But, if you aren't comfortable with that idea, then yes. I'll give you a couple of names."

She bites her lower lip. I hold my breath. We're both in our thirties. Sex is easy. Intimacy, true intimacy, is harder.

I want Dakota to trust me enough to ask me for help. I want her to feel comfortable enough to lean on me. I want her to let me into her life. If she's not ready, then I won't pout. However long it takes, I'll put in the work.

Not going to lie, my heart hammers in my chest as I wait for her answer.

"If it's not an imposition, would you take care of it for me?" she asks, her voice tentative.

Yes! I press a kiss on her lips. "You're never an imposition, sweetness. I will take care of this."

23

DAKOTA

I get a text from Julian at noon the next day. "Talked to Silver's lawyers. They're dropping their demands. Tell Ben to get back to work."

I call him at once. "They dropped their demands? How? Why? What sort of voodoo magic did you perform?"

He chuckles. "No magic required. The optics are terrible, and they know it. You're a successful business owner who made a good faith offer for a building that's been neglected for almost a decade. You are continuing to make good faith moves by making desperately needed improvements to the building. Even after the town council screwed you over, you didn't pull out of the deal. I merely pointed all of that out to Patricia Kane. She knows that she can't take this to court."

"Do you know her?"

"Silver's lawyers? No. I looked them up before I talked to them, of course."

They would have looked Julian King up too, and they would have realized that he never loses. "Thank you, Julian."

There's a smile in his voice. "Anytime, Dakota."

Julian doesn't lose. I can't afford to lose. How is this going to play out?

"About my payment," he continues.

"I can't supply you with ice-cream."

He laughs. "I was going to ask if we're still on for tomorrow."

God, yes. It's been a busy week. I haven't slept with him since Sunday night. I miss Julian. "I hope so. It's supposed to be sunny and clear tomorrow. Want to take my canoe out?"

"I'm a terrible swimmer," he warns me.

"Hang on. I need to take a mental snapshot of this moment. Julian King admits he's not good at something."

"Ha ha, very funny. I'll have you know that it totally derailed my plans to compete in the Ironman."

Trust Julian to want to do a triathlon. Typical. "I have a spare life jacket. This time of the year, it's a must, strong swimmer or not. The water's cold."

WE END up in a secluded bay off Lake Madison. This time, I bring food. We eat hummus and pita and wash it down with cold ciders. "In less than a month," I tell Julian. "This lake will be swarmed with tourists. Enjoy the peace while it lasts."

He flashes me a wicked smile. "Ever had sex here?"

"Are you kidding? This is a small town. Everybody gossips."

He rolls his eyes. "Who cares?"

"Me."

"Do you really?" He lies down, his head on my lap. His hand cups my cheek. "Thank you for bringing me here."

I flush with pleasure. My chest is tight. "Julian, what's going to happen with the contest?" I take a deep breath.

"This all feels like it's too good to be true, you know? I keep waiting for it to fall apart. If one of us gets eliminated tomorrow..."

He puts his fingers on my lips. "It'll work out, sweetness."

"More of your optimism?"

"Sure, if that's what you want to call it. Dakota, I waited for you for a year. A thousand times, I called myself a stupid fool and wanted to walk away, but I couldn't bring myself to do it. Something told me not to give up." He huffs a laugh. "I spent far too many nights jerking off to the memory of our night together." He gives me a sunny smile. "And now, look where we are."

I stare at him. "You waited for me for a whole year?"

"You were worth the wait, Wilde."

I swallow the lump in my throat. "Damn it, King. I don't know what to say to that. I think I might cry."

"No, no," he chides. "I have a far better idea. There's nobody around." He gets up and stretches lazily, and then he sits back down and pats his lap. "Come here, baby."

Every nerve ending in my body sparks to life. "What if someone sees us?"

"There's no road access to this bay," he points out. "The only way to get here is either to walk through a kilometer of mosquito-infested woods, or by water. Look around you. There's not another boat on the lake. If anyone paddles up, we'll hear them." His grin turns smug. "I provided legal services," he points out. "I demand payment."

I'm wearing a skirt. He's in shorts. I look around, and he's right. There's absolutely no one in sight. Quickly, I shimmy out of my panties. "I'm not going to take off my skirt," I tell him. "You'll just have to make do."

"Okay," he says agreeably. He unzips his shorts and frees

his erection. Reaching into his pocket, he finds a condom and rolls it on.

I raise an eyebrow. "Came prepared, did you?"

His lips quirk up. "Are you going to tell me there isn't a condom in that picnic basket?"

I flush. I stopped by the store yesterday and bought a twelve-pack, and yes, I've brought them along. "Fuck you, King."

"Oh, I intend to, Wilde." He crooks two fingers at me. I flip him off but move closer all the same. He puts his hands on my hips and tugs me down, moving my skirt out of the way.

I can't believe I'm going to do this. Outside, where anyone can see us, can see me straddling Julian King's lap. Riding his hot, erect, shaft, grinding myself into him, desperate for the pleasure he gives me...

His fist strokes his cock. Hot anticipation surges through my blood.

Cocaine. Julian King is cocaine, and I'm an addict, and I don't care. I want this; I want him.

"That's my girl," he says. His voice is deep and intent, his eyes, hot with blazing need. There's an honesty about Julian that sucks me in. He's never once tried to pretend he doesn't want me.

Julian King doesn't play games; he doesn't need to.

He's so hard, so big, so erect. I'm wet, ready, my body aching for Julian. I sink into him, and he guides his rock-hard cock into my wet heat, pulling me close. "Fuck, Dakota," he growls, his voice thick and ragged, his eyes bright with pleasure. "You feel so good, sweetness."

I pull myself up, my hands on Julian's broad shoulders, and then I slam back down on his length. He clenches his eyes shut, need written on his face, and a shiver of arousal shocks me.

"Yes," he hisses. "That's right. Seize your pleasure, sweetness. Don't hold back. It's all yours for the taking."

I couldn't hold back if I tried.

His hands grip my hips. I slam down on him; he pulls me in for more. His hips thrust up, and hot pleasure claws through me. He's so deep. My muscles clamp around him. My entire body is tingling, throbbing with desperate need.

I moan out loud, unable to hold back. His eyes meet mine. "Quiet, sweetness," he says, a wicked grin curving his lips. "Someone might hear."

I roll my eyes. "I have it on very good authority that there's no one around."

He laughs. His fingers tangle in my hair, and his mouth meets mine, coaxing my lips apart, demanding and receiving entry. His tongue dances against mine, and I whimper into his mouth as he thrusts into me, hard and deep, taking me, claiming me.

Fuck. This is so good. This is so incredibly toe-tingling, stomach-clenching, mind-bogglingly good. His steel-hard cock drives into me, over and over, driving all thought from my mind.

His fingers pinch my nipples through my t-shirt. They swell in response to his touch, and stick out, erect and pulsing. My breasts feel hot and heavy.

I ache for him.

A familiar spiral begins to tighten inside my core. His cock pounds in and out of my tight, wet, heat, and my orgasm rushes toward me.

He moves his hand between our bodies, and expertly finds my clit. I gasp into his mouth again. "Julian," I whimper.

"I'm here, love."

Love.

A tsunami of pleasure erupts over me. I ride it out, my muscles convulsing around his hard length, my body awash in blazing heat. "That's right," he murmurs, low and firm. "I want to feel every muscle in that tight little pussy clench around my cock. Come for me, Dakota."

I float like a leaf from one orgasm to another. He never stops thrusting, never stops stroking my clit. I shiver and writhe on his lap, shuddering against him, giving in to every sensation, every feeling he's ripping out of me, before I slump against his chest, absolutely drained.

"I am jelly."

He gives me a smugly satisfied male smile. Strangely, I find it charming. It's that damn dimple. So sexy. "I don't mean to alarm you," he says. "But I heard a splash in the distance."

Shit. I jerk off his lap in alarm. "How long ago? You should have warned me."

He shrugs, unrepentant. "You were coming," he says. "It would have been cruel to get in the way of that. Besides, they're nowhere close. Sound carries over water, you know that." He gets rid of the condom, tucks his cock back into his briefs, and zips his shorts, wincing as he does.

Poor guy. He's still rock-hard. That's got to hurt.

He's right, as usual. It takes almost ten minutes for the canoe to near us. A couple is paddling, a couple I recognize. It's Luke and Ruby.

Luke is one of Dom's best friends.

So much for keeping this quiet.

They wave when they catch sight of us. I lift my arm to wave back, inwardly wincing. I guess it was too much to hope they wouldn't see us.

Neither of us say anything until Ruby and Luke are out of earshot. When I'm sure they can't hear us, I groan out loud. "I'm willing to bet they knew what we were doing," I murmur, my cheeks flaming. "By tomorrow, everyone will know that the two of us were hanging out in a secluded beach."

"So what? We're two consenting adults." Julian gives me a sidelong glance. "Does it bother you to be associated with me?"

"No. Not at all." Julian King is the best thing that's ever happened to me. I keep pinching myself, thinking I'm in a dream.

Luke and Ruby are out of sight. And Julian hasn't come, but I did. That's not fair.

"Julian King," I tell him solemnly, lacing my fingers in his. "Will you stick your hot dog in my bun?"

"That's a ridiculous line, Dakota." He kisses me, his eyes tender and loving. "But yes, I will. Get back on my lap. If you don't want to get caught having sex in a public place, you should make me come before your friends come back."

"Cocky asshole."

He kisses my palm. "Guilty as charged."

He slides into me again. I'm so happy I think my heart is about to burst. But underneath, a thread of disquiet coils through me, entangling me in its vicious net.

Tomorrow's Friday. Tomorrow evening, we're going to be pitted against each other.

Again.

What's going to happen then?

24

JULIAN

The idea I had in the back of my mind last weekend has been steadily taking shape. What if, instead of being in competition, Dakota and I worked together? What if, instead of selling one or the other, the new space could sell pizza *and* sausages?

Vicki wants to go back to Toronto. She's looking to sell her share in the Madison Brewpub. Dakota won't be able to swing financing for the buyout this year, but I can.

I could buy Vicki out. Dakota and I could be partners. Three restaurants, especially ones with separate kitchens, would be too much for Dakota to manage without ruining the quality of her life.

But we could do it together.

Dakota's obviously stressed about the contest. I *should* broach the idea to her. I *should* tell her what I have in mind and gauge her reaction.

Yet, I keep quiet.

The truth is, Ward's right. With the exception of Dakota, things have come easy to me.

I'm not saying that I haven't worked hard; of course I have.

But I've never had to be terrified about failure. If I fall, I've always had a place to land. Had I not made partner at BCF, my parents would have moved heaven and earth to hire me at their firms. If Sausage King goes bankrupt, I would still have the cottage my grandmother left me. I'll never have to worry about being too broke to pay rent.

Getting Dakota to date me has been the hardest thing I've ever done. And, now that I have her, now that things seem to be going smoothly, I'm terrified about rocking the boat.

I don't know how she'd react to the idea of us being partners. A partnership is a commitment, one of many I want to make with her.

But even the mere fact that Dakota and I are dating seems like a miracle. I don't want to push too hard, too soon.

When it comes down to it, I'm a pussy. Dakota's not the only one who's terrified about putting her heart on the line.

FRIDAY EVENING, we go through the usual contest bullshit. Checking ingredients, auditing the budget, and then prep.

Rana comes up to me as I chop jalapenos and cilantro for a turkey sausage. "We're keeping a very close eye on things," she says, her voice low. "I've given the producers a heads-up about what happened to Dakota last week. The camera crew has been warned to keep watch for sabotage. If anyone tries to do anything sneaky, we will catch them in the act."

"Good," I say grimly. I'm here for the same reason. If either Hale or Greyson try something, I'll fucking destroy them.

"I also had a word with Sherri," Rana continues. "She's not a fan of Wexler either, no surprise there. We've changed the lock on the kitchen. Sherri's got the key on her at all times. Nobody will be able to sneak back in here tonight."

Rana's taking this situation seriously. That's good.

The prep goes without incident, and I begin to think that things are going to be okay. When we're done Friday night, Dakota comes back home with me, and spends the night at my place, and that's better than okay. "I keep expecting something awful to happen," she admits.

Tell her what you're thinking, King.

"Me too. But everyone seems to be on high alert."

She snuggles against my shoulder. "Ben's ready to get started on the interior," she says. "I had to pay him for the roof and the deck today. Forty thousand dollars. I'm trying hard not to freak out, but every time I think about how overextended I am, there's a tight knot of fear in my gut." She gives me a sidelong look. "You're not as stressed as me."

Tell her, you fucking idiot. Tell her you don't want to take over The Frozen Spoon. Tell her that if you win, the permit is hers.

Fear freezes my words in my throat.

"I guess the King is used to winning, right?" she asks lightly.

I hear the underlying tension in her voice. I squeeze her hand, trying to convey everything I'm too much of a wimp to say. "Things are going to be okay, Dakota."

She's quiet for a long time. Finally, she nods. "I hope so."

SATURDAY IS another brilliantly sunny day. The park is packed with people. A band is playing eighties covers. This weekend, the city gave Cat and Vicki a permit to set up a beer tent. Ale is flowing, dogs and children run around, and everyone looks like they're ready to have a good time.

I get to work, as does Dakota. For a couple of hours, things go smoothly, and I begin to think that Rana's done enough.

And then it happens.

This week, it's not sabotage.

Three buses roll up to the park. People start pouring out of them, and they all make a beeline toward Marvin Hale's unappetizing-looking sliders.

Fuck me with a spoon.

They're plants, of course. It's obvious to everyone that they've been paid off to buy the Friendly Crown's food. And yet, there's nothing we can do about it. There's nothing in the rules that would prevent this from happening.

I catch sight of Dakota's face. She looks stricken. Helpless rage churns in my stomach.

Next week, I'm sure that the judges will find a way to prevent this. But today, we can do nothing. *I can do nothing.* All I can do is seethe as the ticket sales are tallied up.

WHEN IT'S DONE, Rana steps up to the podium. Last week, she'd been all smiles. This week, she's pissed. Her lips are pressed tight, and her hands are clenched into fists. She looks like she's a half-second from punching Marvin Hale in the face.

She's not the only one. The only reason Hale's still standing is because Dakota's family is in the crowds, and she would be mortified if I got into a fight. As much as I want to beat the crap out of the smirking bastard, I can't. I'm never going to do anything to embarrass the woman I love.

Roger Wexler's in the crowd too, looking smug and satisfied. *Fucker.* When I'm done with him, he's going to realize the folly of going up against me. He's going to regret the day he ever messed with Dakota and me.

Rana, Sarit, and Mark Miller are locked in a low-voiced conversation. I wait, Dakota next to me.

Finally, Rana lifts her microphone. "Here are the results of today's contest," she says shortly. "In first place, Marvin Hale from The Friendly Crown."

A couple of people in the crowd applaud, but most people look pissed off. Hale cheated. It feels wrong to reward him for it.

"In second place, Julian King from the Sausage King. Congratulations, Julian. The currywurst was a huge hit."

Fuck. It's between Valentina and Dakota. One of them will be out.

Dakota's recovered from her earlier shock. She doesn't look lost anymore. She looks furious, and I love her for it. *That's my girl. Never stop fighting, Wilde.*

"Valentina and Dakota both made amazing food today," Rana says grimly. "Unfortunately, one of them will have to be eliminated."

I hold my breath. I've represented Fortune 500 corporations at trials worth millions of dollars. I've never been as nervous as I am in this moment.

"Valentina, I'm sorry to say that you were in last place."

Valentina Grayson looks gutted. As terrible as I feel for her, relief floods through me. Dakota's safe.

"That leaves our three finalists for next week. The Friendly Crown, Sausage King, and Dakota's Pizza." Rana doesn't crack a smile. She's furious. "Congratulations. See you all next week."

I turn toward Dakota, bracing myself for her anger, but I've underestimated her. She gives me a wry smile. "Well, that was interesting. I guess we now know who fucked with my sauce."

"Mm-hmm." I need a plan to counter Hale. Next week, if he intends to cheat his way to the permit, he will sabotage both Dakota and me.

"Right now," Dakota says, "I want a long shower and a cold beer." She holds out her hand to me. "Want to get out of here?"

Her mother's in the crowd. Her brother too. Half the town is watching us, and she's holding out her hand to me.

I fucking love Dakota Wilde.

I lace my fingers in hers. Marvin Hale can wait. Tonight, I have more important priorities. Like showing Dakota exactly how much I love her.

Then I see two familiar faces in the crowd, and I suppress a groan. Fredrick and Susan King have terrible timing. "I'm afraid that escape is impossible for the moment," I tell Dakota. "Want to meet my parents?"

25

DAKOTA

So many thoughts are churning through my mind. My emotions are all over the place. My heart races in my chest; my throat is dry. I cling to Julian, but while his touch normally grounds me, today, it does nothing to calm me down.

I'd almost been eliminated. I came face to face with catastrophe. I tiptoed to the edge of ruin, and it's a scary fucking place.

Everything I've accomplished, I've fought for. In the early years, I didn't have enough money to hire a cook; I was the cook. During tourist season, I'd wake up at the crack of dawn and drive straight to the restaurant. I would work from five in the morning until ten at night. I'd take shifts in the kitchen, on the floor, whatever was needed. Seventeen-hour shifts, six days a week, for a four-month stretch every summer.

I'd done that for the better part of four years, until I clawed my way to profitability. I remember how brutally hard it had been. Bathroom sprung a leak? It came out of my profits. Power went out and I had to throw away a week's worth of cheese and meat? I almost missed payroll.

I'd stood there today, waiting for Rana to pick between Valentina and me, and all of it had come rushing back. All that fear, all that panic. I'd stood there today, waiting for Rana to announce which one of us would be eliminated, and I realized how easily everything I've worked for could be ripped from me.

In a flash, it can all be taken away. I can lose everything.

I can't talk to Neil Silver about finding other options; he's already sent his lawyers after me once.

In the meanwhile, while I was fighting for my life, Julian made a currywurst and wowed the crowd. He's in second place. Had it not been for the dirty trick Marvin Hale pulled, he'd have won this round.

Of course. *The Sausage King doesn't lose.*

This situation isn't Julian's fault, but I can't help feeling bitter. He already has a successful business. If he doesn't get the restaurant permit, nothing will happen to him. Mrs. Shepperd still hasn't signed his offer. There is no contract, no deposit.

He could just walk away from it, but he isn't doing that. He's just too damned competitive.

Come on, Dakota. That's not fair. The town council is responsible for this mess, not Julian. He didn't sabotage you; he didn't cheat. Don't make him the scapegoat here.

I'm quiet as Julian tugs me over to meet his parents. He doesn't notice. "Hello, mother, father," he says, shaking the older man's hand. "I didn't realize you were coming down."

Julian's father is tall and distinguished looking, with a head of grey hair and piercing blue eyes. Julian's mother is dressed in beige khakis and a lavender cardigan, and she doesn't have a hair out of place. Both of them have that unmistakable aura that rich people have.

"It was a last-minute decision," his mother says as Julian kisses her cheek. "We ran into Ward at the club. He said you were in a competition of some kind."

"Sausages," his father says, the disgust clear in his voice. "You could have been a partner at Barns Concino Foley, and instead, you're making sausages."

His words pierce my gloom. It's clear that his parents think that he is wasting his time. My temper spikes. With difficulty, I say nothing, settling for squeezing Julian's hand.

"I find it rewarding," Julian says calmly.

"You find it rewarding to cook on stage at some pitiful county fair in front of all these people, like a performing monkey?"

Holy fuck. He's got to be kidding me. What a dick thing to say.

Julian doesn't react. "I was a performing monkey in court too," he replies easily. "This way, at least I feed people."

His father opens his mouth to say something scathing, and I can't bite my tongue any longer. I cut in. "Julian's absolutely brilliant. In just a year, he's become a pillar of the community. He's built a successful business. He supplies half the restaurants in the area. It took me three years to be in the black, and Julian's done it in less than a year. He's effortlessly good at everything he does." I give them a bright smile. "You must be so proud of your son."

His mother's gaze snaps to me. She gives me a 'who-the-hell-are-you' look. "We are, of course, proud of Julian," she says stiffly. She holds out her hand to me. "I'm Susan King," she says.

Julian's arm goes around my waist, and he pulls me

close. "Mother, father, I'd like you to meet my girlfriend, Dakota Wilde."

For a second, shock pulses through me. Then warmth floods in.

Girlfriend.

I like the way that sounds.

Julian feels me stiffen. He gives me a questioning look, and I realize he's nervous. He's actually nervous about my reaction.

I smile at him. The fear that has clamped around me eases its iron grip. I'm his girlfriend. *Things will work out.* Maybe I just need to have a little bit of Julian's optimism.

Both his parents give me speculative looks, and then his mother smiles at me. "It's very good to meet you, Dakota," she says, her tone noticeably warmer. "Julian, I didn't know you were dating anyone."

"I'm dating someone," he replies blandly. "Are you guys up for the day, or you staying? I have a spare bedroom. You're welcome to it."

His father starts to say something about a hotel reservation. My attention wanders. I can see my mother and my brother out of the corner of my eye. Sandra Flanigan is looking at the way Julian's holding my hand, and the expression on her face is intensely curious.

Oh God.

We've just started dating. Julian called me his girlfriend for the first time today. I'm not ready for the meeting of the parents. It's too much, too soon.

I mutter an excuse and head toward my mother. She tilts her head to one side. "Are you dating Julian?" she asks directly.

"Yes, I am."

"You are?" Dominic cuts in.

He sounds disapproving. I frown at him. What the hell? My brother has never once interfered in my life. What's gotten into him now? "I thought you liked Julian," I say mildly.

"Sure, I like King. I don't like the situation. The two of you are pitted against each other in this stupid contest. What's going to happen when one of you loses next week?"

Ah. Dom's my twin; we think alike. "It'll be fine," I tell him, desperately hoping that it's the truth. "Things will work out."

"How?" he asks bluntly. "How exactly will things work out if you lose? How will you make your mortgage payments if you can't expand your restaurant?"

I don't know. Dom's words hit every raw place in my heart with unerring precision. "It'll work out."

My mother is watching me, her keen eyes absorbing everything. Dom takes a deep breath. "Dakota, I'm happy about your relationship. I like King. Even if I didn't like King, it wouldn't matter, as long as you like him. But look at the people he's with. They're his parents, right?"

I nod. "And they're wealthy, aren't they?" he asks.

Dom doesn't miss much. "They're both partners at law firms," I reply tonelessly. "I'm guessing they do okay."

"King grew up rich," he says. "Rich people don't think about money the same way we do, Dakota. Does he even realize how screwed you'd be if you don't win this contest? If he cares about you, why's he still competing?"

I don't have answers to any of Dom's questions. "It'll work out," I repeat stubbornly.

Everything Dominic is saying is right. I am burying my head in the sand. I don't want to rock the boat, because things are really good with Julian. But I do need to have a hard conversation with him.

And then what? Look at Julian's parents. They've dismissed everything he's built. Of course, he's going to want to win. He's going to want to show them what he's capable of.

I don't want him to drop out. This is important to him. But it's important to me too. If we talk, we might be able to find a way forward.

So far, every time I bring up the topic, Julian assures me that things will work out.

But how? I don't see a way out of this mess, and this is too important for me to take on faith. Julian's not the one who's facing imminent financial catastrophe; I am.

My mother puts her hand on Dom's forearm. "Let it go," she says quietly. "Dakota is an adult." She pats me on the back. "We're here for you, honey."

My brother looks mutinous. "I don't disagree with you," I tell him. "Julian and I will sort this out before the finals."

He drops it at last. "Okay."

I watch the two of them walk back to the parking lot. Julian and I are good together. We're both reasonable adults. Surely, we can work this out.

He's been in one relationship that's longer than three months. You've been in zero. Are you sure things will be fine?

I'm about to rejoin Julian and his parents when somebody taps my shoulder. I turn around, and it's Roger Wexler, smiling his oily smile at me. "Dakota. That was close back there."

I'm too tightly wound to be polite. "What you want, Roger?"

"You're going to be in a world of hurt next week," he says. "Neil Silver told me you called him, looking for a way out of your deal. I've always had a soft spot for you, Dakota. I'm going to bail you out. I'll buy the Silver place from you."

Trust Wexler to spin this as an act of charity. "You will, will you?"

"Yes, I will. I heard the message you left on Silver's machine. You don't think you can win, Dakota, and I don't blame you. You're outclassed. Look at the stunt Marvin Hale pulled off today."

I keep quiet and let him talk.

"And then, there's King. He doesn't like to lose." He shakes his head at me. "You're in a relationship with him," he says. "It's cute, the way the two of you were holding hands. You think that'll make him back away?"

"Roger, if you think I'm going to take relationship advice from you, you are very mistaken."

He continues as if I haven't spoken. "King wants to win. Do you know how much money he's poured into the Shepperd place?"

"That was before the contest."

"Is that what you think?" he sneers. "Because the place got a new coat of paint today. The moment Ben Watanabe is done with your job, he's going back to The Frozen Spoon. I saw the permit. They're ripping down interior walls and making the main floor one big open space."

They are?

"You don't have to take my word for it," Wexler continues relentlessly. "Talk to Ben, or, drive by The Frozen Spoon. You'll see what I'm talking about."

My heart clenches. What exactly does Julian mean when he says everything is going to be okay? Is that just some kind of platitude he is giving me in order to soothe my feelings? Does he really think we could continue to be together if he wins the contest and I lose? Is he pouring money into The Frozen Spoon in anticipation of his eventual victory?

Bile rises in my throat.

"I'll make you an offer," Wexler says. "What did you pay for that place? Six hundred? I'll give you four-fifty. Think about it, Dakota. You can either lose more than half a million dollars, or you can be out one hundred and fifty."

I stare at the man. Wexler smirks at me. He knows he has me in a bind.

"Go to hell, Roger."

Anger flashes in his eyes. "You think I'm scum, is that it? You think I'm low-balling you, the way I low-balled Mrs. Shepperd? And you think King's some kind of angel for rescuing Beth Shepperd from my clutches?" He laughs shortly. "He's good at PR, I'll give him that. But at the end of the day, Beth Shepperd is still being forced out of her business."

I turn on my heel and walk away. He calls out after me. "I'll keep the offer open until Wednesday, Dakota. Don't be a fool. There's no other way out."

Julian is still talking to his parents.

I have a pounding headache, and a sudden urge to flee. I walk toward them to make my excuses and get the hell out of here, and then I overhear a snippet of their conversation. "Only one person can win this contest," Fredrick King says. "This is set up for disaster, Julian. You do realize that if you win, you're not going to keep the girl."

"I know what I'm doing," Julian replies. "I don't lose."

That's his answer. Julian King doesn't lose.

Tears filled my eyes; I furiously blink them away. I cannot be here. I cannot go with Julian and have a drink with his parents, and pretend everything is all right, because it isn't.

I need to be alone right now.

26

JULIAN

"Only one person can win this contest," my father says, getting to the heart of the matter with his typical directness. "This is set up for disaster, Julian. You do realize that if you win, you're not going to keep the girl."

I resist the urge to roll my eyes. Yes, of course I realize that. I'm not an idiot.

"I know what I'm doing," I tell him. "I don't lose. This isn't about the contest, and it's not about the permit. That's not what I'm fighting for. Dakota's the prize." I hold up my hand as my mother opens her mouth to give me a lecture about the patriarchy. "And yes, I'm perfectly aware that Dakota is a person with thoughts and feelings, and not a prize to be won. It's a figure of speech. Dakota's important. Everything else is a distraction."

Shockingly, my mother is smiling. "A serious relationship? This is a first for you."

I can't resist needling them. "Yes," I say, my voice bone dry. "It's amazing what I can accomplish when I'm not working eighty hours a week."

My father snorts. We've had numerous arguments about my decision to quit law. They don't approve; they're probably never going to approve. 'Performing monkey' is one of the milder things they've said. But in the end, they do realize that I'm in my thirties, and perfectly capable of making these decisions for myself.

"Why don't we grab a drink?" he suggests. "Ward mentioned that you've done a lot of work on the cottage. I'd like to see it."

"Sounds good. Let's get Dakota, and head back."

I look around for her, but she's nowhere to be seen.

That's weird.

The last time I saw her, she was talking to her mother and her brother. I can't find them either.

Did she leave? She's had a pretty long, rough day. She wanted a shower and a drink. I don't blame her if she isn't up to hanging out with my parents tonight. It's a lot to ask.

But why would she leave without telling me?

Unease simmers in my gut. "Hang on," I tell my parents. "I'm going to look for Dakota."

I call her; it goes straight to voicemail. I walk through the park. I look in the kitchen, but she's not there. I walk up to Vicki, but she hasn't seen her. Mina Ahuja is talking to Mildred Bower, and I interrupt their conversation to ask if either of them has seen her.

They haven't.

I stride to the parking lot; her car is gone.

She left without a word.

I call her again. Still no answer.

I have a very bad feeling about this.

Rana finds me walking back from the parking lot. She catches sight of my face and stops in her tracks. "What's wrong?"

"I can't find Dakota."

She gives me a strange look. "The last I saw her, she was talking to Roger Wexler," she says. "Judging from the expression on her face, I don't think they were having a pleasant conversation."

King, you are the biggest fucking idiot in the world.

No, it wouldn't have been a pleasant conversation. I can guess what Wexler would have said. He would have rubbed her near loss in her face. He probably would have made her an insultingly low offer on the Silver property.

He'd upset her so much that she'd left without a word. *Asshole.*

No, that's not right. This is not on Wexler; this is on me. Roger Wexler is a dick, but that's nothing new. He's always been a dick.

I had a plan. Instead of telling Dakota about it, I let her go into today's contest feeling like she was alone. I let her think that everything she'd worked for was at risk. When she needed me, I wasn't there for her.

All because I was too afraid to fail. Because this time, there's no cushion. This time, if I fail, it would wreck me.

Wexler is an asshole, but in a contest of asshole behavior, I'm the undisputed winner.

I head back to where my parents are waiting. "I have to take a rain check on that drink," I tell them. "I need to check up on Dakota."

My parents have a blind spot about my profession, but they're otherwise pretty mellow. "Of course," my mother says. "Go do what you need to do. We'll probably come down again for Canada Day, but this time, we'll call first."

I drive all through Madison. She's nowhere to be seen. She's not in her house, she isn't in her restaurant. She is not at the Madison Brewpub.

For two hours, I search for her. I drive down every dirt road that leads to the lake. I call her nearly a dozen times. Finally, when the sun is low in the sky, I give up and head back to my cottage.

There's a sinking feeling in my stomach. I have a sneaking suspicion that I've ruined everything.

27

DAKOTA

W hen I'm miserable, there's always one place I go.

To my mom.

The light is on in the house, but I bypass it—I don't want to talk to anyone; I want to be alone—and head to the lake. I clamber on a rock and stare out at the water.

Here's what I know.

Julian isn't actively trying to cause me harm. The worst thing I can say about him is that he's not thinking about what will happen to me if I don't get a permit.

But the blame isn't just on him. This is as much my fault as his.

He's not a mind-reader. Every time we've talked about the contest, he's comforted me by telling me things will be okay, but there's no reason I can't tell him I want more than reassurance.

We're both adults. We both have a responsibility to communicate our needs.

It had been really difficult for me to ask him to talk to Neil Silver's lawyers on my behalf. Asking him to quit the contest would have been so much harder, and I'm not sure if I could have done it.

It's easy to trade barbs with Julian, so much easier than asking him for help. When you ask someone for help, you are vulnerable.

I've made a lot of progress in the last week. After a lifetime of avoiding relationships, I'm actually dating Julian. *He's my boyfriend.*

But I haven't made as much progress as I think I have. When it comes down to telling him how much I need to win this contest, when it comes down to telling him about my fears, my hopes, my dreams...

I can't do it. I'm still afraid to let him in.

I'm a coward.

You know what the worst thing is?

If I'd asked him, he would have walked away from the contest without hesitation.

This isn't Julian's fault. *It's mine. All mine.*

I sit on the rocks for a very long time. I watch the sun set over the lake. Finally, I get to my feet.

I have to talk to Julian. As tempting as it is to hide out here, Julian deserves so much better. He's always been honest with me, and he deserves that in return.

ON IMPULSE, I stop by at The Frozen Spoon.

Roger Wexler's right. Only a month ago, the place had looked in terrible shape. Peeling paint, a broken window, a driveway riddled with potholes... the place had exuded a sense of disrepair.

Now, The Frozen Spoon is transformed. Baskets of flowers hang in the porch. Lights are strung over the deck. Even though it's late, every table is occupied.

Julian really likes ice cream. What was that flavor he'd been eating? Ginger rhubarb, that was it.

I go inside. Mrs. Shepperd stands behind the display case. She smiles at me in greeting. "Hello, Dakota. What can I get you today?"

"Could I get a pint of your ginger rhubarb to go?"

"I'm afraid I've run out, dear." She dips a spoon into another tub. "Try some of the strawberry jalapeno. I just made it."

My heart sinks. *It's not a sign of doom that she's out of Julian's favorite flavor,* I tell myself firmly. *It's just ice cream. Get a grip.*

I take the offered spoon from her. The ice cream is delicious. The jalapeno adds an undertone of spice that complements the sweetness of the strawberry perfectly. "This is really good. Mrs. Shepperd. And the place looks great."

She beams. "Yes, it really does, doesn't it? Julian's such a force of nature. Before he came along, I was stuck. I need to install a wheelchair ramp, and I didn't have enough money to do it, and I thought that it was the end of The Frozen Spoon. Jim was gone, and I couldn't do this by myself. And look at it now."

"Yes," I agree. "Julian has done a great job."

He's done so much work here. He obviously wants this. I can't ask him to give it up for her.

"Are you going to find a different location after you sell?" It's none of my business, I know, but maybe Beth Shepperd would be interested in selling to restaurants. I'd stock her ice-cream at Dakota's Pizza in a heartbeat. "Or are you planning to retire?"

She draws herself up. "Retire? I'm just sixty-six, dear. What would I do with myself once I retire? I've got at least ten years of work left in me."

I blink in confusion. What am I missing?

"I'm not selling this place," she continues. "I thought you knew that."

"You're not? But I heard Julian was buying the place from you."

She shakes her head. "No, that deal is off. He didn't tell you? He came to see me earlier this week. He said he'd changed his mind about being in the restaurant business. He offered me a new deal. I'd make the ice cream, and Julian would do everything else in exchange for fifteen percent of the profits." She smiles at me. "I'm pretty sure he would have done it for ten too."

"He did what?" I ask faintly.

She nods vigorously. "He insisted I get the deal checked out. Told me to call a lawyer, so I did. You know what the guy told me? I'd never get a deal this favorable. Sign it as quick as you can, he said."

"I don't understand."

"Well, reading between the lines, I'd say that the boy is crazy about you, Dakota. I was at Haslam Park for an hour today. Julian looked at you the way Jim used to look at me." Her smile turns sad. "He was my high school sweetheart, you know. The two of us were together for almost sixty years."

Julian doesn't want to be in the restaurant business anymore? He'd withdrawn his offer on Mrs. Shepperd's place earlier this week?

He did this for me.

I have to talk to him. "Could I get a pint of the strawberry jalapeno?"

She packages it up for me. Ice-cream in hand, I drive to Julian's place. His car's in the driveway. He's at home.

I knock. It takes him almost a full minute to answer.

When he sees me, an expression I can't quite decipher flickers over his face. "Dakota."

"Can I come in?"

He steps aside. "Of course."

I walk in. "I stopped by at Mrs. Shepperd's. She told me you gave up the restaurant. Is that right?"

He leans against the door. "Yes, it is."

"Why?"

"Isn't it obvious?" he asks. "I don't want to fight you, Dakota. I don't need the restaurant permit. You do. It was a no-brainer."

I swallow hard. "But you're still in the contest."

"Sure," he responds. "If I dropped out, I'd tip my hand, and then all of Hale's sabotage efforts would be directed toward you." He smiles faintly. "The only person I put my cards on the table for is you, Wilde."

"You told your parents you don't lose. I heard you."

"That's why you ran away? You should have stuck around and heard the rest of what I said. Let's see if I can remember the precise words. It went something like this. 'I don't lose. This isn't about the contest, and it's not about the permit. That's not what I'm fighting for. Dakota's the prize.'"

I stare at him, hope blooming in my heart. "You wanted the restaurant; I know you did. You gave up your dreams. For me."

Laughter dances in his eyes. "What a ridiculous idea," he says. He takes in my expression, and his voice softens. "My dream isn't the restaurant, Dakota. It's you."

Dammit, King. I'm definitely going to cry.

"Dakota, we're a team, you and me. What kind of man would I be if I let the woman I love fail?"

The woman I love.

I blink the tears from my eyes and go up on tiptoe. His

lips find mine. He kisses me, deep and passionate, his hands winding through my hair. "I love you, Julian," I tell him. "I love you so much."

He kisses me again. "That's exceedingly good to hear." His face turns serious. "I'm sorry. I should have told you earlier. If I win, the permit is yours. And if you and me, working together, can't beat that asshole next week..."

We're a team, Julian and me. And together, we will be unstoppable.

I hug him tight. He kisses my nose, his expression tender. It tickles. I giggle, and he smiles. "Thank you for defending me to my parents." His grin widens. "'He's effortlessly good at everything he does.' I *like* the sound of that."

I punch his forearm. "Jackass. Don't you care that you won't win the contest?"

"Because of them, you mean?" He shakes his head. "Dakota, I'm in my thirties. I admit it irritates me that they only have one measure of success, but I've made my peace with it. In their own way, they love me."

"That's very mature of you."

"Yes," he says smugly. "I have hidden depth."

"And there's that giant Julian King ego that I know and love." I hand him the ice-cream. "It's strawberry jalapeno. You should put it away before it melts."

He opens the carton and scoops some ice cream on his finger. "Ooh, this *is* good. Thank you." He quirks an eyebrow. "A long shower, a cold beer, and then bed?"

I snuggle into him, my heart overflowing with happiness. "That sounds amazing."

28

DAKOTA

It's the day of the contest.

Last night's prep went off without a hitch. After we'd cleaned up for the night, Rana had cornered Julian and me. "There won't be any more versions of the bus incident," she'd said. "I have warned the Friendly Crown that if we have any reason to believe that the audience is anything other than genuine, we will disqualify them."

I turn to Julian as we wait to get started. "What are the chances that we can just cook today?"

"Slim to none," he says bluntly. No sugarcoating the truth for Julian King. "Hale is outnumbered, two to one. The odds are not in his favor, and he knows it. Brace yourself, Wilde. It's going to be dirty."

Julian's right. Not to mention that the sliders aren't great, and Marvin Hale is making the same thing three weeks in a row. He shows no desire to leave his comfort zone.

"Brace yourself, it's going to be dirty? That sounds like something you'd say in bed."

He laughs. "Tonight," he promises. "Good luck, Dakota."

I've been nervous about this tournament for weeks now.

But now that we're in the final stages, calm washes over me.

It's because of Julian. It's because we're a team. He won't let me fail.

I love him so much. I don't care which one of us wins today. Because it doesn't matter anymore.

"You too, Julian. Knock them dead."

WE DISCOVER Marvin Hale's first dirty trick as soon as we open the refrigerator.

Last night, Hale had made pickled onions. He'd filled three enormous mason jars with them, and he'd placed them in the refrigerator.

Overnight, they've exploded.

My tomato sauce, which was in a covered saucepan, is safe.

But Julian's sausages were in a container on the bottom shelf, covered by paper towels.

They're ruined.

The vinegar has soaked through the paper towels and has pooled in the base of Julian's containers. Worse than that, pieces of glass are everywhere.

Pickles don't explode, especially not quick pickles like the one Hale was making last night. I don't know what Marvin Hale added to his vinegar to cause this reaction, but I know one thing with absolute certainty.

This is deliberate.

Rana swears when she sees the carnage. "What the hell?" she snarls.

Marvin looks unconvincingly apologetic. "Fuck, man. I'm so sorry. It shouldn't have exploded like that. I don't know what happened."

Sure. I believe that.

Julian stares at his sausages for a long time, his face expressionless. "Can you salvage this?" I ask him.

He shakes his head. "It doesn't matter, Dakota. I'll sort this out. Get back to work."

Fuck.

Anger pulsing through me, I go back to my station. I turn my oven on to preheat it, and punch down my dough. I'm furious on Julian's behalf. He'd worked really hard on those sausages. He'd made a traditional calabrese last night, and then he'd worked on a chicken, artichoke, and basil sausage, and finally, he'd made a vegetarian version, with tofu, cilantro, chipotle, and lime.

The only one left undamaged is the vegetarian sausage. It's undoubtedly delicious, but I know Madison. Attitudes are slowly changing, but most of the residents regard tofu with suspicion.

Poor, *poor* Julian. He doesn't deserve this.

He's talking to Rana, Sarit, and Mark. I overhear snippets of their conversation. Julian looks unhappy, but finally, he nods curtly.

"What's going on?" I ask him when the camera crew isn't within earshot.

"The damn budget," he says. "They're allowing me to buy sausages, but if I use my product, I'll have to pay full retail price. That's why I've been making my sausages in this contest. Meat is cheaper."

"What can you do?"

He grimaces. "Buy less. I'll only be able to feed a hundred people." He looks into my eyes. "I'm dead in the water, sweetness. You're not. Kick some ass."

I'm so furious I'm shaking. I roll out the dough, add sauce, toppings and cheese.

Then I open the oven.

It's dead cold.

Of course, it is.

This, Hale couldn't have managed on his own. This bit of sabotage has got to be courtesy Roger Wexler.

There are three sets of ovens in the space. I move over to the empty station that Don Mazzio had used a couple of weeks ago.

His oven won't work either.

That only leaves one option. There's only one other station that has an oven.

Julian's.

Julian King likes to win; everyone knows that. Wexler and Hale must have assumed that Julian wouldn't trade places with me.

They're idiots. Even if Julian genuinely wanted to win, he would have given me the working oven. And then he would've beaten everyone anyway, because that's what he does. Unlike Marvin, he doesn't need to cheat to win.

"What's the matter?"

"My oven's out."

"Use mine," he says calmly.

I start to gather my stuff, and then I freeze. What the hell am I doing? Why does one of us have to win, and the other has to lose?

It's complete bullshit. If we're a team, we both need to win.

Of course.

We're a team.

Why aren't we acting like one? Why aren't we competing *together*?

Julian's already in a partnership with Mrs. Shepperd. There's no way the thought hasn't occurred to him. Why hasn't he broached it to me?

Probably because he doesn't want to pressure me.

"Did I ever tell you Vicki wanted to sell her share of the Madison Brewpub?" I ask him as I move my stuff over. My heart is in my throat. "I've been thinking about it, and I don't think I can manage all three spaces. I think I should look for a partner."

His eyes laugh at me. "Do you?"

The camera is pointed in our direction. They're filming us. Then there's most of the town of Madison in the park, watching everything we do. My mother's in the crowd. So are Dominic and Cat. Vicki. Luke and Ruby. Teresa Barbini and her son Gino. Tim Pollard. Elise and Trey.

I don't care.

I'm perfectly aware that I'm going to be the topic of gossip in Madison for months. I don't care about that either.

All I care about is Julian King.

"I don't want to do this without you," I continue. "Dakota's Pizza doesn't just have to serve pizza. That's just a name." I bite my lower lip. "It could also serve sausages."

"It could," Julian agrees. "If that's what you want."

"That's what I want." I close the distance between us. I ignore the cameras. I ignore the crowds. "Will you be my partner, Julian?"

His smile feels like the first rays of the morning sun. "I'd be happy to."

I put my arms around him and hug him tight. "To be honest," Julian whispers in my ear. "I thought it'd be too much commitment for you."

He knows me pretty well. "Any second now, I'll start to freak out. Until then, savor the moment."

His chocolate brown eyes are warm and filled with love. "Oh, I intend to."

I feel so very lucky. "I'll have my lawyer draw up a

contract." I wink at him. "Oh wait, you're my lawyer. Julian, will you draw up a contract?"

He grins. "I feel compelled to point out that you should get an independent opinion."

I roll my eyes. "Screw that," I announce. "I trust you. Shall we shake on it?"

"I'd rather kiss on it."

Sounds good to me. I stand on tiptoe and press my lips to his.

In the background, the crowd cheers. I barely hear them. I'm in Julian's arms, and I'm kissing him, and everything is exactly as it should be.

Rana is Madison's social media manager, and she's sensing views, likes, and retweets. We might even go viral. Mark Miller is a television producer. He realizes we've created a perfect reality TV moment.

Chef Sarit Onruang's beaming too, but I think that's because she's a secret romantic.

"We don't want to compete against each other," I announce to the judges. "We want to combine teams."

"No," Marvin Hale snaps. "They can't do that. I protest."

"You're not in charge, Mr. Hale," Rana responds icily. She's still mad about his stunt from last week. "Mark, Sarit? Thoughts?"

"I'm okay with it," Mark Miller says.

Chef Onruang nods. "Me too."

"Excellent." Rana rubs her hands together. "Only one of you can cook; it wouldn't be fair otherwise. And we'll still have to sort out your budget. But yes. One team."

I turn to Julian. "I've got this."

He kisses me again. "I know you do, Wilde. Go kick some ass, baby."

WE WIN, of course. After that public display of affection, the crowds were rooting for us. It wasn't really a fair contest. Everyone loves a good love story, after all.

At the end, when the winner is announced, and Julian and I have bowed and waved to the cheering crowds, he turns to me. "About that contract," he says, a wicked glint in his eyes. "Want to go pound out the details?"

"*Pound.* Very funny, King." I wink at him. "I went by the store yesterday," I whisper into his ear, trying not to blush. "I bought some lube."

For a second, pure shock flashes across his face. *It's remarkably satisfying.* Then his eyes flare with heat.

"You did, did you?"

"Mm-hmm." I flutter my eyelashes at him. "I have a hot new boyfriend. He's fascinated with the idea of anal." My cheeks feel hot. "And I thought, that maybe tonight, we could, you know, go there."

He starts to laugh. "Go there?"

Really? He's going to make fun of me? I glare at him. "King, do you want to stuff your sausage meat into my..."

He kisses me before I can finish that sentence. "Dakota," he says against my lips. "I beg you. No more sausage puns."

I give him a mock-astonished look. "No more sausage puns? What will we talk about instead?"

He puts his hand on my elbow and steers me toward his truck. "We'll figure it out."

Julian and I, we're never going to be a restful couple. Our life is going to be filled with snark, banter, and adventure.

It's going to be amazing.

EPILOGUE

DAKOTA

Victoria Day

I t's a holiday weekend, and all three restaurants are packed.

Teresa has chosen today of all days to get the flu, and so Julian and I are dancing around each other in the kitchen. So far, we've collided into each other twice. There's been an unfortunate flour incident, and the front of my apron was soaked with tomato sauce.

All part of a day's work.

I wouldn't change my life for anything.

It's been a really good year.

Right after the permit was approved, Ben Watanabe worked in record time to get my new restaurant ready. Opening day went off without a hitch. Every table in both the original space and in the expansion had been occupied.

Some of that was because of the contest. The First Annual Madison Cook-Off aired on television, and became a sleeper hit. Tourism in Madison is up fifteen percent as a result. Half the town is happy, and the other half grumbles bitterly about never being able to find a parking spot. No surprises there.

We were never able to prove that it was Roger Wexler who sabotaged the ovens. It doesn't matter. In the fall elections, he was defeated handily.

The new councilor, the one who took his seat? Beth Shepperd. The moment she'd announced her decision to run, Wexler knew he'd lose. Everyone in town had heard about the way Roger tried to exploit Mrs. Shepperd. Everyone had remembered, and, even better, they'd turned out to vote. Wexler is still Madison's biggest property owner, but he can no longer use his power as a councilor for personal gain. For the next four years, he can't bother us.

My mother loves Julian. His parents love me. "Honestly," Julian grumbles. "They like you more than they like me."

He might be right. They're still sore about the fact that he quit his fancy law firm. Ah well. They'll eventually get over it.

I thought it was bitterly unfair that Valentina Grayson had been eliminated from the contest because of the way Marvin Hale had cheated. La Mesa's food is horrible, but Valentina was a really good cook.

However, that story had a happy ending too. Mr. Alvarado, who owns a Mexican restaurant on the outskirts of town had been in the crowd the first day, and he'd tasted her cooking. He found her after the contest and offered her the head chef job in his kitchen. Julian and I are addicted to her tacos, and we eat at Casa Alvarado at least once a week.

So really, all's well that ends well.

After the lunch rush is over, I kick Julian out of the kitchen. "Ward's here. He's come down this weekend to hang out with you. Go talk to him. I'll handle things here."

I expect a protest, but Julian just kisses me. "Don't be too long," he says. "Samir and Kevin can handle things."

He's right. Both my line cooks are calm and unflappable, and perfectly capable of handling things without me. "I might be a bit of a control freak."

He laughs quietly. "Shocker. I'd have never guessed."

"Sarcasm is the last refuge of a weak mind," I tell him loftily.

His lips twitch. "Personally," he says. "I find Dostoyevsky a colossal bore." He kisses me again, his hand cupping my neck and pulling me closer. "Hurry."

My nerve endings tingle from that kiss. My body throbs in anticipation. "I won't be long."

VICKI STICKS her head in the kitchen. "Do you need a hand?" she asks.

I wave her in. "Yes, desperately. Want to stay for the summer? You could run the place, and Julian and I could take a vacation?"

She walks in and puts on a hairnet and an apron. "Very funny," she says. "Sorry. You're on your own."

She's laughing as she says it, but there are shadows in her eyes. "What's wrong?" I ask her as I make a quick roux. How the hell did we run out of *alfredo* in the middle of the lunch rush? Don't ask me. At the end of the long weekend, I'm going to have to go Gordon Ramsey on someone's ass. This is prep, damn it. We shouldn't be doing it in the middle of lunch service.

Vicki sees what I'm doing, and helpfully chops a bunch of parsley, her movements smooth and practiced. "Guy trouble, of course," she says wearily. "What else?"

"Tell me about it."

"Will's getting married."

I stop adding cream to the sauce and turn to look at her. "Will, the guy you've secretly been in love with for more than ten years, is getting married?"

"I haven't been in love with him for more than ten years."

I beg to disagree. I've heard her talk about him. From what I've pieced together, the two of them have been friends for the longest time. They've never been single at the same time. The windows have never lined up.

"Have you told him how you feel about him?"

"No, of course not. He's engaged, Dakota. This isn't a sitcom. It's not romantic to break up a relationship; it's a dick move." She takes a deep breath. "There was this one moment where I thought we had something..."

"Then what happened?"

"It got complicated. Now, he's engaged to someone else." She shrugs helplessly. "It's just so sudden. I didn't even think he was dating anyone."

She's going to cry into the parsley, and then I'll have to throw it out and start over. I rescue the herbs before that happens. "Tell him how you feel."

"I don't think I can do that."

"Weren't you the one that told me I needed to have more faith? Didn't you say you wanted what Dom and Cat have?"

She doesn't reply. I want to push, but I take one look at her face, back off, and change the topic. Life comes with no guarantees. Vicki will either figure this out or not. As much as I hate it, there's nothing I can do. "Did Julian tell you the latest sales numbers?"

Julian bought out Vicki's stake in the Madison Brewpub. Well, I guess we both did, since we're partners. He took over their operation, tweaked the menu, and kept things on track. Sales are up twenty percent. Of course. The guy's never run a restaurant before, and he wanders in and makes everything better.

She forces a smile on her face. "As soon as I walked through the door. I like Julian, Dakota, you know I do. He's a great guy. But twenty percent? I wanted to punch him."

I laugh out loud. I know exactly how Vicki feels. "Welcome to my world. If he wasn't my boyfriend, he'd be the most irritating guy in the world."

He's the best guy in the world.

Julian is often smug. *Of course, he is.*

I call him a cocky asshole a lot. *Of course, I do.*

We are deliriously happy.

Of course, we are.

EPILOGUE

JULIAN

"You look really nervous, buddy." Ward gives me a lazy grin. "Don't worry. She'll probably say yes. You haven't done anything to annoy her this morning, have you?"

Over Christmas, Dixie finally broke up with Charles. Ward, never one to waste a perfectly good opportunity, had swooped in immediately. The two of them are now together. On the surface, they seem like polar opposites. Ward's an anally tidy accountant, and Dixie is a personal chef who seems to exist in a perpetual state of controlled chaos, but they're actually great together. They balance each other out.

Dixie's come down this weekend too. She's chatting with Vicki, who is also in town, visiting Cat and Dominic. It's one hell of a party. Everyone's here.

I just want ten minutes alone with Dakota.

"I bumped into her, drenching her with tomato sauce."

Ward laughs. Asshole. "You think this is funny, do you?" My eyes narrow. "One day, you'll find yourself in my shoes. Remind me to laugh in your face."

He pats my back. "You really not sure what her answer is going to be?"

He has a point. I'm pretty sure she's going to say yes. We're had conversations about getting married, and we're on the same page about this. Neither Dakota nor I want children, but we both believe in marriage. The guys that propose on the Jumbotron at stadiums when they have no idea what their girlfriends' reactions are going to be? Those guys are fools. This is the biggest decision of my life. Of course, I'm going to make sure my girlfriend feels the same way I do.

Doesn't mean I'm not terrified.

FORTY-FIVE MINUTES LATER, Dakota emerges from the kitchen and collapses into a seat. "Tell me the worst of the lunch rush is over," she groans.

"The worst of the lunch rush is over." I wink at her. "Did you remember to eat, Wilde?"

She gives me a disbelieving look. "Did I look like I had time to eat?"

Excellent. Walk into my trap, sweetheart. "I packed a cooler for us. Think you can get away for ten minutes?" I give her my best persuasive look. It works on juries, it works on judges, and it works on her.

"Ten minutes."

"Maybe twenty," I hedge.

She makes a face. "Go get some fresh air," Ward urges her. "If there's a crisis, they'll call you. And we're not going anywhere; Dixie wants to try everything on the menu. We'll still be here when you get back."

I take back all the mean things I've ever said about Lewington. He's a stand-up guy.

"Okay." She gives me a brilliant smile. "Let's go eat."

We drive out to Haslem Lake. It's a little chilly. Warm enough in the sun, but the end of May is not picnic weather in Madison. We have the place to ourselves. I open the cooler and hand her a hot dog. "Big enough for you, baby?" I tease.

"I'm starving. I'm going to devour your meat, King." She leans against me, resting her head on my shoulder. "Do you know, it's our anniversary today? Two years ago, we hooked up for the first time." She giggles. "Is it weird that I'm celebrating the day we hooked up?"

"It's not weird at all. But, on that note..." I pull the small jeweler's box out of my pocket. "If you want to make it official?"

Her eyes go wide.

I flip it open and extract the ring and hold it out to her. "Will you marry me, Dakota Wilde?"

She doesn't say anything. I fill the space with nervous words. "The ring was my grandmother's. It's a sapphire. I thought, since you don't really like diamonds, that this would work better. My father sent it down. But if you don't like it, we can change it."

She holds up her hand. "Stop talking, Julian. I'm trying not to cry." She throws her arms around me and hugs me tight. "The ring is beautiful. Of course, I'll marry you."

I let out the breath I didn't know I was holding and slip the ring on her finger. It fits her perfectly. *It's like it was meant to be.*

Dakota brushes away her tears. "So, what you're saying is, you want to stuff your sausage in my casing forever."

"That is awful."

She giggles. "It is awful. Hang on, I'm going to think of another one."

"Dakota," I say, kissing her to shut her up. "Stop the awful puns and kiss me back."

She's mine. I'm hers. For the rest of our lives. I am the luckiest guy in the world.

I don't mean to brag—okay, who am I kidding, I'm *totally* bragging—but the King *always* wins.

THANK you for reading Dakota and Julian's story! I hope you love them as much as I do.

WANT MORE ROM-COM? If you enjoyed meeting Cat and Dominic in this story, don't miss **Hard Wood**! It's a full-length steamy romantic comedy featuring a hot-as-hell carpenter (Dominic!), a spunky, sassy brewer (Cat!), carpenter puns (*screw and hammer, tongue and groove, nail*

gun), and loads of steam. Flip the page for an extended preview of Hard Wood.

DO YOU ENJOY FUN, light, contemporary romances with lots of heat and humor? Want to read *Boyfriend by the Hour (A Romantic Comedy)* for free? Want to stay up-to-date on new releases, freebies, sales, and more? (There will be an occasional cat picture.) **Sign up to my newsletter!** You'll get the book right away, and unless I have a very important announcement—like a new release—I only email once a week.

A PREVIEW OF HARD WOOD BY TARA CRESCENT

Cat Milnick's Summer To-Do List

1. Get my new brewpub up and running.
2. Ignore the wickedly handsome Dom Wilde and his kinky furniture.
3. **No more carpenter puns.** *Screw and hammer. Tongue and groove. Nail gun.*
4. Focus on the beer.
5. Remember: If I fail, I'll have to go back to working for my evil ex-boyfriend.
6. Don't get turned on when Dom calls me his little spitfire in his sexy, smoky growl.

And above all, don't get too attached to his...*ahem...***'hard wood.'**

∼

Dom:

Alone in my workshop, I turn up the volume on the radio and resume work on the set of custom cabinets I'm making for Jan Patterson's new kitchen. I lose track of time. Three, maybe four hours pass. The radio's hyped-up morning show hosts finish their shift, and a slower, mellower mid-morning crew takes over, playing classic rock. I'm humming along to Led Zeppelin's Kashmir when the door bursts open, and a woman marches in, indignation oozing out of every pore in her body.

I look up automatically when the door opens. Then I stop what I'm doing and look at the woman again. She's petite. Shoulder-length blonde hair, tinged with pink. Her eyes are dark and stormy, her nose is as cute as a button, and her lips are full and lush.

She stalks toward me, her breasts bouncing under her thin t-shirt in a mesmerizing, distracting way. I have to force myself not to stare. I can see the dark outline of her nipples underneath the white cotton, and fuck me, that's hot. She's not classically beautiful, but my cock is extremely intrigued.

"Hi." I turn off the power sander, take off my safety glasses, and lower the volume on the radio. "Can I help you?"

She folds her hands over her chest, pushing out those glorious tits. "Yes," she snaps. "You can *certainly* help me. You can explain what the hell a sex chair is doing in my brewpub." Her eyes flash fire. "Is this some kind of a joke? Because it's really not funny at all."

It takes me a second to catch up. "You work at the brewpub?" Fuck. Gino Barbini, Chaos Lord, strikes again. He had two pieces of furniture to deliver, and somehow, he's managed to mix them up. If he dropped off Zach's sex chair in the brewpub, then the countertop is probably already in Bainbridge.

I could call Gino and chew him out, or I could laugh at the ridiculousness of the situation. I choose the latter. My lips twitching, I survey the indignant woman. "Come on. You don't think it's a little bit funny?" I wipe my hand on my jeans and stick it out to her. "I'm Dominic Wilde. It sounds like my delivery driver, Gino, screwed up."

She shakes it reluctantly, her hand tiny in mine. "Cat Milnick. Where's my bar?"

Hello, kitty. "Is that short for something?"

Her eyes spit fire at me. "Catherine. Not that it's any of your business, Mr. Wilde."

She's wound up so fucking tight. I wonder what she'd look like after she makes love. Strands of her pink hair spread out on a pillow, her full lips curled in a smile, her body soft and sated.

My cock hardens even further, and I mutter a curse under my breath. This is insane. I'm not a teenager. I enjoy women, but I've never pictured someone in my bed so readily. I haven't been this painfully turned on in a long time.

"Call me Dom, please."

"Fine. *Dom.*" There's a defiant edge in her voice. "Where's my bar, Dom?"

Knowing Gino, it could be anywhere in Ontario. "My best guess? Bainbridge."

"Bainbridge?" She snatches her hand back, and her voice rises in pitch. "You've got to be kidding me. That's hours away from here."

I'm not seeing the problem. "Relax," I say, trying to pacify her. "I'll call Gino, and he'll get your bar back."

"The same Gino who dropped off that *chair* in my pub. Or whatever it is." She sounds incredulous. "Smack dab in the middle of the restaurant, where anyone walking by on the street can see it."

Every time she mentions the chair, she moves her weight from one leg to the other. She's turned on. Her nipples are pebbled, and her cheeks are pink, and she can't meet my eyes.

I bite back my grin. The truth is, I have a pretty good read on the woman standing in front of me. She might dye her hair pink, but that's the extent of her rebellion. As fascinated as she is by my chair, she'll never act on her curiosity. Like Teresa Barbini, she'll fantasize about BDSM from the safety of her e-reader.

A devilish urge comes over me. "Whatever it is?" I chuckle. "You had it right the first time, Catherine Milnick. It's a sex chair. If you're interested, I'd be more than happy to show you how it works."

∾

Click to keep reading Hard Wood. It's a standalone romance with a guaranteed HEA and absolutely no cheating!